The Beginning of Our Ending

SYDNEY RENEÉ

I want to send a special thanks to everyone who played a part in making this book great. I appreciate all the help and support. You all know who you are and you're the best!

Author Note

The Beginning of Our Ending is a story I hold dear to my heart—about second chances, the importance of communication, friendship, and making it through difficult decisions. The topic of abortion and miscarriage is mentioned throughout this story and can be triggering, so take a break if you need to. I've been there, and I know reliving loss can be painful.

On a happier note—there will be happy endings, but sometimes, you have to make it through the storm first.

Table of Contents

The Beginning of Our Ending

<u>1</u>
Tests and Regrets

Saturday, October 9, 2010
Skye

Today isn't starting the way I planned. Here I am, rushing to the store to buy a pregnancy test. It's the last thing I want to do, but my intuition tells me not to wait a minute longer. It's only been a day since I've missed my period, but that is one day too long, especially for a woman like me—whose red sea never fails to flow.

I can't forget to mention the week of on-again, off-again spotting. At first, I thought nothing of it—assuming Mother Nature was around the corner, ready to knock at my door any second to wreak havoc on my life for an entire seven days, but my cramps were becoming way too intense for them to be early signs of PMS, for me at least.

Nope.

My body is reacting to something else.

The cravings, the mood swings, and the oversleeping. Normal for most, but highly unusual for me, mainly the hours spent in my bed dead to the world.

If you look up 'early bird' in the dictionary, my ebony-coated face, with the deep right dimple and Bambi's eyes, is probably staring back at you. My internal alarm wakes me up at 6 a.m. every day, but lately, I've been sleeping past nine and taking involuntary naps all hours of the day. Thank goodness I'm in business for myself because I'd be fired by now.

Then there's the obvious.

The lack of contraception. I should know better. It's not like my mother didn't talk to me about the birds and the bees. I just turned 25, for goodness' sake. *Fuck yeah, I should have known better. Been taking birth control at least.* Unfortunately, sex can be more blinding than love, mainly when it feels like you're living out a scene from your favorite romance novel—hot, sexy, passionate, and downright nasty.

Escaping the moment is nearly impossible. Having to stop in the middle of a half-naked make-out session to remind your man to get a condom or to make sure to pull out isn't always as easy as it seems. With my man, I admit it was something I couldn't bring myself to remember. The chemistry was always so intense that I'd melt into him every time, and when we finished, I'd savor the feeling of him inside me while we fell into dreamland.

I've dreamed of being a mother since I was a little girl. While other girls were preparing to be the first female president, lawyer, or veterinarian, I counted the days until I could become old enough to start a family. Every picture I drew included one— me, my husband, and our children. I had a chunky little cabbage patch doll I'd bring everywhere, pretending to be its mother, feeding it, changing it, and loving it like a real human being. I've spent my life preparing for motherhood. Now that my dream may become a reality, I'm terrified.

Babies may be cute, but nothing about raising one will be easy. It won't always be sunshine and roses. My and my mother's relationship has shown me that countless times.

Skye: *Pulling up to the store now.*

Lance: *Text me as soon as you get the results. I have to get back to work before my supervisor catches me taking another break.*

The store is a few blocks from my apartment, and once I pull into the parking lot, uneasiness washes over me.

Maple, California, is a small town with about 20,000 people. I live in a lively area of town, with blocks of small restaurants, cafes, boutiques, exercise and art studios, and the busiest convenience store. I'd hate to run into anyone I frequently see, especially one of my clients. Most are out of state, but my faithful first are still around.

I started my own business, **Written in the Skye**, helping small businesses and upcoming authors with website builds and offering writing and editing services. I'd say

I'm pretty damn good at what I do, too. It pays the bills and more. I wouldn't trade it for anything, especially a career at my father's law firm.

Getting out of the car, I rush into the store, heading straight for the pregnancy tests, hoping to avoid drawing any attention to myself. The last thing I want is to be the center of anyone's gaze or gossip, so I quickly scan the shelves, searching for the most reliable test kit while trying to keep a low profile. Black shades and a dad hat could have helped disguise me, but I was in a rush.

Why are there so many?

My head explodes, trying to figure out which ones to grab. It's not like this is my first time taking a pregnancy test, but my brain is currently fried due to the stress and embarrassment of possibly seeing someone I know. Also, I don't want to have to come back in here.

Grab them all!

Looking around, I notice no customers present, which is a relief. I may be a grown-ass woman, but I feel like a teen, afraid the world will find out I've been busting it wide open while telling my parents I'm still a virgin. It's embarrassing—more embarrassing than the time I went to buy condoms from the gas station, and the cashier didn't shy away from telling the whole line, which was full of men, my business.

I quickly scan my surroundings one last time to avoid the same embarrassment. After creeping around the store for a few more seconds, I make a beeline for the counter.

Victory, I think, until I hear a familiar voice beside me—a voice that used to comfort me.

"Damn, you sure move on fast," he says, and I know he's referring to all the tests spread out over the counter.

I jump in front of them, attempting to hide the evidence of what I know he'll register as an act of betrayal. Instead of turning to face him, I keep my head down as the clerk rings me up.

Of all the places and times, why did it have to be today?

"Ayla, I know you can hear me," he says, tapping me on the shoulder.

I hate when he calls me by my middle name, but I also love how smooth it rolls off his tongue—beautiful and demanding.

In a past life, I would have answered him immediately, like a dog that runs around in excitement when they hear their owner call to them, but I'm no longer his. I can't jump just because he speaks my middle name with authority. I can't give him that satisfaction, but If I don't answer him, there's no telling what kind of scene he'll cause in this store. Running into him is already humiliating enough.

He'll surely tell my best friend how he saw me and how I pretended he was a ghost. Though at this exact moment, I wish he'd vanish. I won't hear the last of it if that information gets back to her.

Feeling guilty, I slowly turn to face him.

"Funny seeing you here." I slightly smile at the man I once had the privilege of being with for four years. Those were some beautiful years.

"Is it? I stay right around the corner. It was bound to happen one day."

"At this moment, I find it...interesting that out of all the people in the world, you happen to be the one person I bump into," I say, facing the clerk to pay.

I should have been worried about running into the man I was supposed to spend my life with, not the guy from the laundromat I talk to about true-life crime or the instructor from the hot yoga class I attend...occasionally.

"It's quite the coincidence. Running into the woman I once hoped to have children with picking up pregnancy tests. It's shocking," he says, rubbing his temple, a sign of irritation—I immediately recognize.

"I can't help but feel a little appalled that you've chosen to start a family with someone else so soon," he comments. "I mean, is the breakup still not fresh to you?"

Welp, this is awkward. Looking over at the clerk, I grab my bag and walk around my ex.

"I gotta run," I quickly say and rush out of the store. This isn't the time. It may never be, but today sure as hell isn't.

"Maybe I'll see you around," I hear him yell from afar.

Hopefully, you don't.

Lance: *Have you taken the test yet?*

Skye: *I'll let you know as soon as I do. I just left the store. Heading home now.*

Entering my one-bedroom apartment, I immediately head towards the bathroom. I take out four pregnancy test sticks and use them one after the other. The silence in the room is deafening, and I can hear every little sound.

While I wait for the results, I try to distract myself from my earlier encounter with Desmond. I can only imagine how he must be feeling right now. To say I feel like the worst person on earth would be an understatement.

I don't recall him looking that fine when we were together. He was attractive, but something about him has changed since I last saw him. The nastiest thoughts went through my head the moment his juicy lips parted to speak—they'd indeed look delicious between my legs, covered in my nectar.

Focus Skye. There might be another man's baby inside of you, and all you can think about is sex with your ex.

With bated breath, I pick up the first test, and within a second, my suspicions are confirmed—*pregnant*. I pick up another stick, and the two pink lines are vibrantly staring me down, and the next reads *pregnant* on the screen. I didn't bother looking at the last test because I knew the results would be identical. Despite the evidence, I still can't believe what I see. There's no way.

But there is.

Placing all the tests on the counter in a line. I take a photo and then send Lance a message:

Skye: *You're going to be a dad.*

~

Lance immediately called me after I shared the news with him. The excitement in his voice vibrated through the phone. He practically shouted to the mountain tops, telling everyone he could that he would soon be a father. I'm pretty sure I could hear him crying.

Regardless of how he was feeling, I found myself in a state of shock. My dream of being a mother was coming true, but suddenly, I was skeptical about the whole situation. I imagined this happening entirely different. This isn't what I dreamed about. *He* isn't the man I dreamed about. But dreams never stay the same.

Don't get me wrong, Lance is an outstanding man—any woman would be lucky to start a family with him. Currently, every quality about him is remarkable. He works, provides, adores his mother, is faithful, and the sex—full of passion. The thing is, we haven't been together for a long time.

We met while I was out one night with my best friend, trying to mend my broken heart. He ended up charming me right into a relationship. That was almost eight months ago.

I haven't had any reservations during our time together, but I can't ignore that we jumped into a relationship immediately after I officially ended things with my ex, Desmond. I hadn't even bothered to check if Lance was seeing anyone at the time or fresh out of a relationship, but that wasn't part of the mission I was on.

Either way, evaluating whether we are emotionally and financially equipped to raise a child together is necessary. It's a decision that requires careful consideration and planning. I want to be fully prepared for the responsibilities and challenges.

You should have thought about that before you told this man to cum inside you. Foolish!

Discussing a family in the heat of the moment and creating one are two different things. I can barely take care of myself. I'm making good money—**Written in the Sky** isn't a failing business, but I'm a woman with expensive taste who wants to keep living that way. I can only guess the amount of money I'd need to bring in once a baby is added to the picture, especially if I'm going to spoil it the way my parents did me…or at least used to.

My mom, like the bitch she is, forced my dad to cut me off when she doesn't work herself. She's a glorified housewife who does nothing except judge me for the choices I make, especially if they aren't the ones she made for me. My dad only expected her to raise me into an intelligent and respectful young lady, which she did, but she hates that I didn't get to that point doing everything her way.

My dad, a retired lawyer, still sneaks money into my account here and there. No matter how old I get, he still looks out for me. He doesn't hesitate to provide whatever I need—the upside of being an only child. Mom would blow a gasket if she knew how much and how often he put an allowance into my account.

Speaking of my mom, I would be planning an early funeral if she knew I was pregnant. Lina Rose becoming a grandmother to a baby conceived by anyone other than Desmond Walker is just unacceptable. The mention of my boyfriend's name makes her sick.

She's been disapproving of our relationship from day one. The first time I introduced them, her face said it all—disgust. He tried to hug her, and her body language screamed, *get away from me.* Not to mention, she couldn't stop saying Desmond's name at the dinner table. *How's Desmond doing? I miss talking to him. Oh, Desmond is so sweet.* It was so fucking rude and one of the reasons I haven't introduced him to the rest of my family. He hasn't stepped foot around my mom since that night. We were supposed to spend the night there, but Lance felt so disrespected he insisted we drive the four hours back to Maple.

My dad, on the other hand, was more than kind. Despite his love for Desmond, he

welcomed Lance with open arms. As long
as I'm happy and not being mistreated, he's
happy for me. I never have to worry about
disappointing him or feeling anxious when
he calls my phone or we enter the same
room.

I wish it could be the same with my
mom.

~

My mind is consumed with doubt as I sit
up in bed. Lance is sleeping beside me
peacefully, but I can't bring myself to
snuggle against his warmth so I can do the
same.

Upon receiving my message, he eagerly
rushed to my apartment. He couldn't resist
the urge to come to rub on my nonexistent
belly. Lance walked through the door
bearing my favorite treats—Sour Patch
Kids, hot Cheetos, beef jerky, and peach tea.
He also brought me flowers.

I love the joy the news brought him, but I wish he would calm down a bit. I'm already overwhelmed, and I just took the tests.

What if I miscarry? What if I don't want this, and then he hates me?

"What are you still doing up?" He asks, rolling over and wrapping his arm around my waist.

"Sorry. I didn't mean to wake you. I can't sleep."

"Is there something on your mind?"

Yeah, there is, my insides scream. *I don't think I want a baby. I don't want your baby.*

I don't dare to utter those words out loud. My mind is racing, and I need time to reflect and decide my next move. There are multiple paths that I could take, and I need to weigh all my options.

"Earth to Skye," Lance says, sitting up, waving his hand in my face as I stare off into the land of babies.

"I'm doing great, thank you."

"I didn't ask how you're doing. I asked if there was something on your mind." He takes hold of my chin, turning my face to him.

"There's nothing on my mind. Today was just eventful, and I'm not as tired as I thought. Too many naps, I guess."

I didn't fix my lips to tell him I ran into my one true love while in the store. We never talked much about my relationship with Desmond. All he knew was that I had gone through a "bad" breakup and was looking to move forward.

"Do you want to watch a movie and eat some of the snacks I brought you?"

"I appreciate the offer, but I'm good," I reply, settling comfortably in his embrace. "This is all I need."

2

The Beginning

Thursday, January 19, 2006

Skye

Most people don't believe in love at first sight, and I was one of them. That changed when I met Desmond Walker at a college party. I'd been attending Maple University for three years. For the most part, I spent all my time with my head in the books, building my freelancing business on the side and trying to live up to my mother's expectations—socializing for fun wasn't on that list, but it was a new year. A new year meant new things, and that meant saying yes more.

I was never interested in going out to bars and attending house parties, especially in a small town like Maple, a town I didn't even know existed.

Attending a small-town university was nothing exciting, but it was better than going to a college of my mother's choosing—double points for being able to remain by my best friend's side.

Emily had a big-city mindset but a small-town heart. She wanted to be somewhere that felt like home, and when she found out about Maple, it was the only option for her, mainly because her boyfriend Jordan was already going there. Jordan attended the same high school as us and graduated a year before we did. I wouldn't be left in the suburbs four hours away with my mom or at some college my mom wished she had gone to, so I applied and was ecstatic when I got in.

After hours of being badgered by Emily about attending a frat party, I agreed to go with her. My papers and homework had already been completed, and I had just finished putting the finishing touches on the campus's online newspaper.

When we left for the night, I hadn't planned on falling in love the second I walked through the door. The universe, aka Emily, clearly had other plans for my 2006 school year.

People always talk about how they met their partner in college and lived happily ever after, but to me, it was just something people said. It was an adorable story to tell. A story I refused to believe...besides Emily and Jordan's. They'd been dating since high school. They were the exception.

In the time I had been living in Maple, not one guy had caught my eye, and damn sure hadn't captured my heart, but when I saw Desmond, my perspective changed drastically. The guys here were okay looking—a little too country for my suburban upbringing, but Desmond—that man was everything, and to think I could have met him a few years prior.

Emily was always trying to get me out of my dorm so I could meet someone. She suggested I meet one of Jordan's friends, whom he'd met during his first year of college, but I instantly declined. I didn't want to know his name, where he was from, or what he looked like. She had forced me on a blind date with one of his friends once before, and it was a complete disaster. I had to pay for everything, and the bastard never thanked me. He didn't even bother calling me. After that ordeal, I objected to being around any of his friends again, and Emily respected my wishes...until the night of the party.

Once we walked through the door, she spotted Jordan. She nudged me and pointed to the guy standing next to him.

"That's the guy you refused to let me introduce you to," she said. "He and Jordan are like the best of friends now. Don't you think he's cute?"

He was.

Desmond stood at 5'8 with a slender frame that lent him an air of elegance. His deep brown eyes were mesmeric, entrancing anyone who gazed into them—me. His face was smooth, with subtle freckles that could only be noticed by those who looked closely. But I found his smile, complete with dimples, most endearing. He was breathtakingly handsome, as if he had been custom-made for me.

As soon as our gazes met, I was overtaken by an indescribable sensation that seemed to pull me in his direction. All my thoughts and surroundings faded into the background as I became completely fixated on him. The intensity of the feeling was so strong that I yearned for it to envelop me entirely, never to let me go.

Some call it lust, and trust me...he was worth drooling over—these lips of mine wanted to touch every inch of him. But lust isn't what it was. It was love. Not that I'd ever been in love before, but I knew from the moment we locked eyes this was the "You'll just know" moment everyone spoke of.

I had never experienced anything like it. The feeling was unmistakable. It wasn't just a fleeting physical attraction that I wanted to act on—it was something more profound—magical.

There was an intense desire to introduce him to my family, my extremely critical, stuck-up family—to share my life with him and only him. I could see us traveling the world together, exploring exotic destinations, and experiencing the wonders of different cultures. I could see us getting married and starting a family, building a life filled with love and adventure. It was like a dream come true, and I knew deep down in my heart that he was the one for me. If that isn't love, then I don't know what is. The feeling was so strong. I couldn't ignore it. I needed him and was willing to do whatever it took to make it happen.

"It's nice to finally meet you, Skye," he said when Emily dragged me over to him.

I looked around the room and then back at him. "You...you know my name?"

"How could I not? Your friend right there brings you up every chance she gets. For a second, I thought you were one of her imaginary friends." He laughed.

"Well, it's nice to meet you—"

"The name is Desmond."

"Well, it's nice to meet you, Desmond." I reached out to shake his hand, and he pulled me into him instead. His embrace was nice and warm. "And if I were you, I'd think I was imaginary too. I don't get out much."

"I've seen you around."

"You have?"

"Yes, I have, but you always seem busy, and I heard about the last clown they introduced you to. I wouldn't want to meet any more of this guy's friends either." He pointed to Jordan, and we all shared a laugh.

As the night went on, the happy couple snuck off, and Desmond and I continued to talk. I felt my heart race with excitement and anticipation for the future I'd already planned out within the few seconds of staring at him. We drank, danced, and laughed all night. Before I knew it, we were leaving the party together, and it felt like the world was ours for the taking. We spent every moment together after that.

<u>3</u>

Keep Quiet

Sunday, October 10, 2010

Skye

I find myself lost in thought, reminiscing about a past life I thought I left behind until it came staring me dead in the face.

It was one of the toughest days I've experienced when I officially ended things with Desmond. Suddenly, waking up and deciding that a relationship with the only person I saw myself growing old with, wasn't worth saving devastated me. Yet, I didn't bother trying to hold on. Once I chose to let go, I couldn't look back.

I never got closure. I didn't allow myself that luxury. Fear of having made a mistake in letting him go held me back. I was afraid he wouldn't let me back through the door. Had I gone begging for another chance, I doubt he would have let me in, so I stayed away.

Instead, I occasionally visit him in my dreams. There's a sense of reality in them that brings me comfort, but I can't help but feel guilty for having him on my mind while lying next to another man—the man I left him to be with.

It's a constant battle between my heart and mind, and I'm unsure if I'll ever find a resolution that won't hurt everyone involved, specifically Lance.

I caused Desmond so much pain. I subjected him to humiliation. I abandoned him without so much as a backward glance. I can only suspect he sought refuge at Jordan's house and spoke ill of me behind my back. You would think Jordan's known Desmond longer than he has me.

I'd be cold-blooded to put Lance through that same humiliation.

"Good morning," Lance says, rolling over to kiss me. "How'd you sleep?"

"Great."

"You must have because I expected you'd be up and dressed by now."

"Blame it on Poppy." I giggle.

"Poppy? You gave the baby a nickname already?" Lance asks.

"Not purposely. I'm assuming I'm four weeks pregnant, which means the baby is as small as a poppy seed."

"I get it," Lance responds with a chuckle.

"Speaking of babies, are you going to tell your mom the news, or is she going to be pissed?

I was hoping he wouldn't bring up the topic. I had already decided that I wouldn't tell my mom anything about the pregnancy, not at this point, anyhow. The thought of being judged by her was just too much to bear. Her words played in the back of my head:

You bet not let that boy get you pregnant. You won't even be with him for that long. What do you see in him in the first place? He won't be a part of any family I belong to.

I never had to deal with this in my relationship with Desmond. It might have been the only time she was somewhat nice to me. She still felt a certain way about me doing everything opposite of what she wanted me to do, but she was confident in the man I'd chosen to be with. Something about him reminded her of my dad.

My mom had everything planned out for my life, and I went against all of it, but with Desmond, she could see her dreams for me finally being fulfilled—a beautiful home, a dream wedding, and a slew of grandkids to dote on, for a fee, of course.

In her eyes, Desmond was the perfect match for me. So, you can guess her reaction when I ended up with Lance instead. To her, he was the guy who ruined her daughter's future of happiness and stability—something my dad provided and continues to provide her with. The woman wanted to disown me, and she probably would have if my dad hadn't intervened.

On top of that, I still need to book an appointment with my doctor, find out how far along I am, and determine if the bleeding I'm experiencing is normal. I read up on implantation bleeding, but if that's what is happening, it should have stopped by now.

"Let's not get too ahead of ourselves. It's still very early," I say, getting up. "Anything can happen."

"It won't."

He has no idea about the complexities of pregnancy and the workings of a woman's body. It hasn't occurred to him that I could lose the baby suddenly—no explanation. Even if I don't, there are other potential dangers of childbirth, like the baby facing health issues, not to mention how neglectful doctors can be when it comes to black women.

"You don't know that," I raise my voice slightly. "Let me make an appointment with my doctor, and I beg you not to say anything to anyone until I'm at least three months pregnant."

"Three months?"

"Yes, three months," I say, walking toward the shower.

"What about my mother?"

"Especially not your mother," I respond quickly. Mrs. Evans will scream it to all the church folk and her little neighborhood walking group. She and her son don't know how to keep a secret, especially when they're overjoyed.

"Fine, I guess I can wait," he says, disappointed.

"I'm serious, Lance," I say, piercing him with my eyes, "keep quiet."

"I won't say anything."

"Thank you!"

<u>4</u>

Real Love

Sunday, October 10, 2010

Skye

Once Lance left my apartment for work, I called my best friend to arrange a therapy session over some good food.

I know I swore Lance to secrecy, but I had to confide in Emily. Lucky for me, she owns the most divine brunch location in town. The place is always buzzing with activity, but after shutting down at 1 p.m., it becomes our haven for therapeutic sessions, where we bare our souls and unburden ourselves.

"Bitch, what are you thinking? A baby?" Emily takes a sip of her drink. "I thought Lance was just a rebound. A fun fuck. A temporary relief until you came to your senses. Not a potential baby daddy."

"He was until he wasn't. I wasn't expecting him to be more than a one-night stand. There was something there that I felt was worth exploring. I'm sure you understand."

"Well bitch, you explored alright," Emily says before pouring herself a shot of tequila. "And do not compare your feelings for him with the ones I have for Jordan. I've been with him since high school. You've known this man...not even a full year yet."

"Oh, shut the hell up. You're just mad we can't go on those corny-ass double dates anymore," I say, eyeing her shot.

Once her brain registered that I wasn't leaving Desmond after moving in with him, she immediately began to schedule couples' activities for us: paint classes, picnics, cherry picking, movies, karaoke, and whatever else she could come up with.

"Bitch you can't have any, and you're damn right I'm mad we can't do those corny-ass dates. My man kicks me to the curb whenever Desmond comes around because of you." Emily takes her shot back and slams it down on the table.

Desmond and I weren't officially over when I got involved with Lance. We were

going through the motions and decided it'd
be best to take a break. A break was all it
was supposed to be. Our relationship
progressed so quickly that by year four, all
we were doing was arguing or not
communicating. We were letting the days
pass us by—no attempts to fix our issues.
He'd go to work at his gym or hang with his
boys, and I'd stay home building my
business and trying to stop myself from
going crazy. The lack of communication
was depressing, and I was no longer living
in a bubble of love but one of isolation.

I knew the only way our break would
work and for me to regain some of my
independence was to move out of the
apartment we shared. Granted, I didn't
move far. I found myself in a beautiful
apartment complex about two blocks from
where we shared *his* apartment on
Lavender Lane. I loved the quiet yet busy
neighborhood we were in and couldn't see
myself any place else.

About three weeks after moving out, I
was missing Desmond like a crackhead

misses their fix—I craved him, and being away from him was eating away at me. Every muscle in my body wanted to rush to his place to work things out, but I refused to give in that quickly, to act as if nothing had changed between us.

Emily saw my agony and decided she had enough of me lying on the floor, surrounded by tissue paper and junk food. One night, she dressed me up and took me out on the town. At one of the many bars we strolled into, I met Lance—chocolate, handsome and full of confidence. The man was fine, and I did not object to spending time with him...after a slight push from Emily. Our one-night-stand turned into eight months, and now, possibly 18 years, stuck with one another.

"If anyone is to blame, it's you," I say, rolling my eyes at Emily. "Miss, he's cute. If you didn't force me out the house that night, I'd be back with Desmond by now, not pretending to be happy with another man, and you'd be having a ball on those corny-ass dates you miss."

"Hey now, don't blame me for your lack of self-control. I told you to dance with the guy. No one told you to lock him down. And what do you mean by pretending to be happy? You've seemed pretty damn happy to me up until you took those pregnancy tests."

I didn't intend to let those words slip. Duh, I'm happy. Maybe not the happy I'm used to, but I'm content. Things with Lance are easy. We vibe, talk, and spend a lot of quality time together when he isn't working. We don't even argue. What woman wouldn't be happy?

"I didn't mean it like that. I'm happy with him. I just think, *what if*, sometimes."

"You wouldn't have to think about the what ifs if you just stuck to the plan. You were supposed to have a little fun to get your mind off Desmond, and then in a month or two, you were supposed to realize this holiday away from Des was just that...a little break." Emily thumps me in the forehead.

"The sex, it was the sex." I blurt out, letting a laugh slip. "It was magnificent. Healing. How was a bitch only supposed to sample it once?"

"Is that all? The sex was soooo good that you had to leave Desmond? Give up on a lifetime of *real* love."

"Honestly?" I ask, fiddling with my fingers.

"I asked, didn't I?"

"It's out of this fucking world. I think that dickmatized bullshit people talk about is real. I didn't believe it, but I'm legit obsessed with it," I say, slightly mortified. I can't believe I became the girl who let dick ruin a practically perfect relationship.

"All those years with Desmond, you mean to tell me he wasn't fucking you right." Emily leans in, curious.

"I didn't say that, but fucking the same man for years can get boring. You know they get comfortable. But before he got lazy, I lived on that dick and enjoyed every inch," I say, biting my bottom lip.

"Welp, I did not want to visualize that, yet here I am." Emily covers her eyes and puts her head down.

"Since we're having an honest conversation," I say, looking over at Emily, "I've only stayed this long because I wanted to prove to everyone this relationship could last."

"Everyone? Or your mean ass mom?" Emily rolls her eyes.

"You know how that woman can get."

"No disrespect, but *that* woman is a fucking bitch. She has been since the day I met her. You have so much more going for you than being Desmond's woman. I love him, but your success has nothing to do with that man. She acted like the world would end when you told her about the breakup instead of doing what a mother should do."

"I know," I say, trying to cut Emily's rant short, but that fails. Once she gets started on my mother, there's no stopping her.

Emily would come to my house frequently when we were younger. Most of the time, my mom would be out on her little shopping trips, doing everything she could to avoid being home with me, but when she was home, Emily always had to listen to her negativity:

Skye, put that ice cream back. Your hips are getting a little too wide.

Skye, you should straighten your hair more often.

Skye, stop spending time with that girl and focus on preparing for SATS.

Skye, didn't I tell you nothing good comes from hanging around girls prettier than you?

Oh, but her final straw came when I brought her into Emily's restaurant, and she proceeded to embarrass me and disrespect her establishment. It was the only time I've witnessed Emily lose her shit. There wasn't much she could say to my mom about how she treated me because I wasn't saying anything, but she wouldn't let my mom disrespect her, not even a little.

"All she had to do was comfort you, but instead, she belittled you and told you, you wouldn't be shit. I will never get how she ended up with a man as loving as your father." Emily pauses to give me room to speak, but I have nothing to say. "And Skye, since this is a place of honesty, it sounds like you don't want the relationship or the baby. You said it yourself. You're just trying to prove your bitch of a mother wrong."

Tears fill my eyes, and it's the only response Emily needs. She knows me well enough to know I'm stuck between two men and a baby.

"So why not just end things and move on with your life before you're stuck living with regrets?" Emily asks.

"And have everyone hate me after they've told me I told you so?"

"Fuck what everyone has to say. They aren't the ones carrying a baby by a person they don't truly love," Emily says.

"I do love him."

"But are you *in* love with him?"

$$\underline{5}$$

Girl's Night Out

Saturday, January 30, 2010

Skye ·

"It's only been three weeks, Em," I say, mindlessly searching for my Slim Jim as I lay on the floor admiring the ceiling. It's the only thing I've looked at for weeks. "Can't I just lay here and pity myself?"

"No, you cannot." She takes hold of my right leg and drags me toward my room. "What did you break up with him for if you were just going to lay in the dark all day feeling bad for yourself?"

"Sometimes a girl just needs a break."

"And sometimes a girl just needs to get pretty, have a few drinks, and possibly get laid," she says, stretching out her hand to help me off the floor. "He's the one that should feel like shit. You asked the man for a break and then moved out. The holidays just passed…the man fell in love with you in January, and you broke his heart the same month years later."

Pulling my hand away, I help myself off the floor. "Way to make me feel better." I hadn't even thought about timing when I told Desmond I needed my space. That probably explains the rain cloud that's been following me around everywhere.

"I'm sorry." She backs up. "I promise I won't say anything else about it."

"Yeah, whatever. I still don't want to go out. Let me stay home and eat my life away."

"That's what we're not about to do. I have to look at Desmond's pitiful face whenever he comes to see Jordan, then I come to visit you and have to look at the same damn face. Can't you two just be miserable together?"

"I'm getting in the shower now." I run to the bathroom and close the door before she follows. I cannot hear her talk about me and Desmond for another second. *Is she my best friend or his?*

All I have to do is let her doll me up, put a few drinks in my system, and then dance like there's no tomorrow. *What's the worst that can happen?* I asked for a break so I could find myself again. Maybe tonight will help me do just that. I deserve to let loose. To have a moment of happiness. To let go of the pain I've been carrying around with me. If I still feel bad tomorrow, I can say I lived for a night.

Once I'm finally out of the shower, I let Emily put very little makeup on me. I opt for a simple outfit—a black crop top, black skinny jeans, black heeled boots, a choker, and oversized hoop earrings.

"Ready," I inform Emily.

"Yay!! Girl's night out," she squeals.

~

"Can we go home now?" I whine.

"Skye, you're not having fun with that fake little two-step you're doing. It's not working for me," she says, pulling me to the side of the bar. "Why don't you stop ordering Shirley Temples and get a real drink instead?"

"You noticed?" I laugh.

"Yes, I noticed, and since you want to play, I'm about to order some shots. I bet that'll loosen your sad ass up." Emily waves over to the bartender, and we're three shots in before I can count to ten.

"One more for the road," Emily says as the bartender slides two tequila shots our way.

"Do I have a choice?" I lift my shot glass—softly clinking it against hers and then take it back.

Pulling me through the small crowd and out of the bar, we walk up the street to one last spot. I know the shots are kicking in because I suddenly have this urge to talk loud, and I need to pee. Once we get to the next bar, I head straight to the bathroom. *I can't go another minute without relief.* Checking myself in the mirror, I re-adjust my curls and my titties in the black crop top I'm wearing, then apply a new layer of lip gloss.

Stepping back onto the dance floor, I immediately spot Emily bouncing to the beat of "Ice Cream Paint Job." We lock eyes and go back and forth, reciting the lyrics as I dance to her.

"I love this fucking song."

"Me too!" Emily yells, and we start to laugh. "Those shots hit us, didn't they?"

Giggling, I respond, "Most definitely."

As music from the early 2000s starts to play, the crowd enters the bar and onto the tiny dance floor. The nostalgia of being a teenager hits me the more I and Emily sway to the music—laughing at the outrageous dance moves I was attempting to do. The only thing that will make this a night to remember is dancing on the bar Coyote Ugly style.

"You want some water? I need some water," I whisper into Emily's ear.

"Yes. All this dancing has me feeling dehydrated. Is this a sign of old age? I can't get old. Not yet." She fake cries.

"Girl, come on." I pull her to the bar. "Can we get two bottles of water, please?"

"How about a real drink?" The bartender says flirtatiously.

Giggling, I respond, "Just water. Thank you!"

"Don't look too hard, but the chocolate dude in the pinstriped button-up at 6 o'clock won't stop staring."

I turn my head and pretend to scan the crowd but immediately lock eyes with him. "Is he looking at you or me?" I quickly turn away.

"You," Emily answers, "and he's walking over here."

"How do I look?" I ask nervously.

"Thirsty." Emily hunches over, laughing.

"Okay bitch, it wasn't that funny."

"Sorry to intrude on this little moment you two are having," the mystery man from across the room says as he steps between me and Emily, "but I think you look gorgeous, and I would love to dance with you." He extends his hand, waiting for my answer.

"Yes, say yes," Emily mouths from behind him. "He's cute."

"I don't dance with strangers." I glance up at him.

The man is like a tree. A fine, tall tree. Oh, or a fine glass of wine. I think I like that better. I catch myself starting to let out a laugh but stop. *Focus!*

"For all I know, you could be some kind of serial killer who goes to bars in small towns looking for your next kill. I'm bite-sized. I'm like the perfect victim."

"Bitch, you watch too much television," Emily yells out, and the three of us start laughing.

"If it makes you feel any better, I spend most of my time with my mom or at the job," he informs me.

"Um, I don't know if that helps your case. Most serial killers are mama's boys."

"Wow. You're hilarious." He smirks. "I like it."

"I promise you I'm not that funny," I respond.

"Well, at least give me the chance to find out for myself."

This guy is persistent.

"If I can't get a dance, can I at least have your name?" He asks.

"It's Skye," Emily answers for me. "Her name is Skye."

I cut my eyes at Emily before showing her my beautiful smile. I know she's trying to get my mind off Desmond for the night, so I can't be upset. It's not like he's some hideous giant she's trying to ship me off with. She's just trying to be a good friend, and the night has turned out to be fun.

"Nice to meet you, Skye. My name is Lance, and I'm a Gemini."

"You're one hundred percent an axe murderer, but since you're so handsome, I guess one dance won't hurt," I say, taking his hand. "Try to keep up."

6
That's Wild

Sunday, October 10, 2010

Desmond

"That's wild to me. How could she throw away everything we had for a nigga she hasn't even known but for a hot second? She doesn't even know that nigga for real, but she out here willing to have his baby and shit."

I spent four incredible years with Skye Ayla Rose. I loved everything about her—how she talked about the people and things she cared for, the ground she walked on, and how she always went out of her way to make me feel special. Every weekend we spent together was full of quality time, creating new memories, and enjoying our favorite activities. I cared for everything on her days off, so she didn't have to lift a finger. I cooked, cleaned, and provided for her, showing her new things and places. We almost had it all, living every couple's dream. But we have one tragic hiccup, and she decides to abandon our plans and leave me behind.

We could have made it through that heartbreak if she wanted to.

I thought I was over this shit, but seeing her buy multiple pregnancy tests brought up some unresolved feelings, ones I thought I buried. I know I wasn't perfect, but I wasn't some cheating asshole who did her dirty.

"What did she say when you saw her?"

"Bro, she tried to act like she didn't hear me when I know damn well she did because I put some extra bash in my voice, but I played it cool, made a little jokey joke when my mind was saying, 'bitch what the fuck are those for?' Not that I'd ever call her a bitch."

"You hella funny. You gotta chill." Jordan laughs as I pace back and forth in his living room. "And you know damn well her little ass would have popped you in the mouth if you called her a bitch. I would love to see her little ass take you down."

"Are you on my side or hers?" I stop in front of him, folding my arms over my chest.

"You want me to answer that?" Jordan smirks.

I wave him off, continuing to speak, "Then she had the nerve to say funny seeing you here or some shit like that as if we don't live around the corner from each other."

Picking up the beer from the coffee table I'm pacing in front of, I say, "That shit is wild."

I had been at Jordan's house venting about Skye for hours. Despite having known Skye before coming to Maple, he'd become a brother to me over the years. I appreciated him for listening to me pour out my heart about this woman. I know I was getting on his nerves, but he stuck it out. Thank goodness Emily loves me like a brother because she might have made him cut me off for the sake of her friendship with Skye.

I thought I was cool off her. Figured I had gotten over the way she broke up with my ass. I had finally reached a point where I didn't want to end it all, but then I just had to run into her.

It was a given that our paths would cross again, but somehow, we managed to steer clear of each other despite only living a few blocks away. Jordan and Emily went to great lengths to guarantee we were never in the same vicinity. Our usual gatherings were officially canceled following the end of our relationship. Emily *did* try to fight me over that shit. She's a sucker for a double date, and apparently, her life is in shambles without them. I told her to blame that shit on her friend, and she almost choked me out.

"Don't get mad at me, but that shit is kinda funny. You two have managed not to see each other since the breakup, partly due to my baby and me being so accommodating. Then, not even a year later, you're watching her buy pregnancy tests." He puts his head down and laughs. I don't find the shit funny at all. "That's the shit you'll find in one of those movies they loved having us watch. Straight up comedy."

"I'm happy my suffering brightens your day," I say, walking over to the couch to rest my legs, "but that shit is like a *fuck you* from the universe, if you ask me." I kick my feet up.

"Maybe this was the sign you needed. I know you've been hoping that she'd come to her senses one day, and I ain't gon lie, I miss all the shit we used to do, so I've secretly been hoping she comes back around, but I know you are not trying to play dad to another man's baby," Jordan responds.

"So, she is pregnant?" I say, planting my feet on the ground and hunching over. *My chest hurts.*

"Yeah." Jordan places his hand on my shoulder. "Sorry, bro. Emily told me all her tests were positive, but don't go saying shit."

"Yo, have you met this nigga or what?" I ask defensively.

"Relax. Skye might be my longtime friend, but you should know got damn well I'm not letting that man stroll into any place I'm at. If she ain't coming with you, it's a no-go," Jordan reassures me. "Emily is still pissed about having to hang out solo with Skye, though. She thought you guys would be back together by now."

"Nigga me too, but she left my ass in the dust."

7
Confirmation

Monday, October 18, 2010

Skye

Leading up to the week of my doctor's appointment, Emily had given me a lot to think about. I still didn't have an answer to her question: *was I in love with Lance?* Like real love—the kind all the R&B Divas sing about—that Mary J. Blige "Be Without You" kind of love.

I guess the answer is no, *right?* If I were, I would have answered instantly. I wouldn't be considering ending my relationship. Being with Lance is easy. It's peaceful and a bit more entertaining. He makes me laugh. The way Desmond used to in the beginning. He makes me feel wanted, even when we aren't speaking. His ability to be vulnerable is another reason it's been simple to keep this thing of ours going. Most men don't give you that. So, it isn't just the sex that pulled me in.

Lance is an experienced security professional. He works for several companies in the inner city. He prefers to work the graveyard shifts as he finds it more lucrative than a typical 9-5 job. He says the balance he needs is the flexibility of sleeping during the day and avoiding the hassle of dealing with people. Whenever he talks about work, it sounds like he doesn't get paid to do shit but sit around and watch movies on his laptop during downtime.

I visited him a few times when we first started dating since it seemed like I could never get much of his time, but driving into the city incredibly late at night isn't my favorite thing to do. Those times I did go, I always made sure it was worth it. On one of those visits, we pulled out a blanket and fucked on the couch after he made his rounds. Thank goodness the security cameras didn't work in that building because he would have gotten fired the next day.

I wonder which shift would be the best for us once our little one arrives. I know I'll need all the help I can get. The night shift seems like a great option. Plus, he would have plenty of time to spend with me and the baby during the day. As for living arrangements, I can't help but overthink and worry about the future.

I need to stop thinking so much and get ready for this damn appointment.

~

I never imagined my doctor's visit would be as lengthy as it was, especially since I was only five weeks pregnant. The whole routine was uncomfortable, and I was glad Lance wasn't with me. No matter how much he begged, I couldn't say yes. I thought it would be a quick blood test, a brief ultrasound to check for anything unusual, and then I would be on my way. But boy, was I in for a surprise!

After being weighed and checking my blood pressure, I got undressed for an ultrasound, and it wasn't what I had expected. I expressed my concern about the constant bleeding to my doctor, so she performed a vaginal ultrasound, which revealed a sac and a minuscule dot. Although nothing else was visible, my doctor reassured me that there were no signs of a miscarriage or an ectopic pregnancy.

I'll need to schedule a follow-up appointment in a month to hear a heartbeat and get a clearer view of the baby.

"Will the father be coming to your follow-up appointments with you?" The doctor asks. I'm sure not out of concern but pure nosiness.

What does it matter if he comes to my appointments or doesn't? It's not like he will be the one pushing out the baby.

"Um, I'm not sure. Maybe a few. He wanted to come today, but I told him it would be a waste."

"The first few appointments are usually fast, as there's not much to see this early on, as you saw, but it's nice to hear that he wants to be involved. Most young women come through here with no support system, and I hate to see it," she says as she types a few things into her laptop. "These guys knock up these girls and are nowhere to be found after. It's unfortunate."

Sadly, that does usually end up being the case—little boys, who think they're men, getting hit with the reality of becoming a father after that pregnancy test comes back positive. Suddenly, we should have been smarter and being told they aren't obligated to do shit since they aren't the one who has to carry the baby. *You could have got an abortion*, they like to throw in your face, but it's not always that way, and she has some fucking nerve for assuming it is.

There are other reasons a man might not be around. He might have passed away.

The dude could have turned out to be an abusive piece of shit that she couldn't take being with any longer. Maybe *these* young girls were taken advantage of.

It could be so many things, and this woman is sitting up here judging every woman—women of color, I'm sure, that comes through her examination room.

I wish my old doctor didn't get promoted and moved to another hospital.

"Or they just might not be comfortable having someone around…you know, in case there's bad news," I respond, annoyed.

"Whatever the case may be, I'm happy to hear you have someone who wants to be by your side," she replies, placing her hand on my knee. "These papers are for you, and I'll see you next visit. You can get dressed and get that scheduled right out front."

What a bitch! I think as she exits the room.

My next appointment will not be with her. Her ass is way too comfortable stating her opinion when it wasn't even asked.

Black doctor me, please!

8
Don't Keep Me Waiting

Monday, October 18, 2010

Lance

Skye shared some big news with me—a new life coming into the world! I never thought what it would be like to be a father, but the moment she told me she might be pregnant, I prayed for it to be true—a chance to carry on my last name with a woman I could see being my wife.

We haven't had any serious conversations about the future, except when I'm deep inside her. Having a family with her would be beautiful. Starting our own traditions and learning new things about ourselves and our children as they grow. Living in a home that's always full of laughter and love. It would be reminiscent of the house I grew up in.

She asked me to keep the pregnancy a secret for now, and I'm not sure why, but rest assured, I won't share this information with anyone…but my mom, *of course.*

I can't hide something this beautiful from her, not even if I wanted to. It's a blessing.

Unlike Skye's mom, who hates me without giving me a chance—I know my mom will welcome this news with open arms. She loves Skye and has been eager for me to find a woman to settle down with.

I've never been one to bring just any woman around, but there was something different about Skye. She's a breath of fresh air and nicer than most of the women I've dated—jokes a lot, but I enjoy it. She doesn't complain about how much time I spend with my mom, which makes me like her even more. I don't hear any of that mama's boy talk from her.

When my dad suddenly had a heart attack and passed away, my mom's well-being became my main concern. Working and taking care of her became my priority. I didn't know how she was going to cope with his death—living in their home without him. She's done well for herself, though. I can honestly say I've never actually seen her shed a tear. Every day, she manages to wake up with a smile. Maybe the memory of their love keeps her going; I want that kind of love.

I hope I can get that from Skye.

From the moment we met, I felt a deep connection that I couldn't explain. The night I met her, you wouldn't have even known she was going through a breakup. She was so beautiful and carefree. It might have been all the drinks I had consumed that night—I was still going through some shit— grieving my father, but she looked like she was glowing. Nothing was about to stop me from approaching her.

Despite how fresh her breakup was, it was me she chose, and I'm committed to doing everything within my abilities to make sure she continues to pick me. Ole boy wasn't doing what she needed him to, obviously.

Walking up the steps, I knock on my mother's door. I make it a point to visit her before heading off to work. One of our weekly traditions is indulging in tacos every Tuesday, which we both look forward to. We attend church and enjoy Sunday dinner afterward, provided my work schedule allows it. Skye is now a part of that routine.

I appreciate her dedication. She knows how happy it makes my mother and me. On occasions when I can't join, Skye takes the initiative to keep my mother company.

Opening the door, my mother snatches the flowers from my hands. "I'm so happy to see you, my wonderful son. Are these for me?"

"Isn't it obvious," I say, kissing her cheek?

I follow my mother into the kitchen and retrieve a vase from the top of the cabinet, placing it on the counter for her. She's too short to reach the higher shelves but insists on putting things up there. It's almost as if she did it intentionally to force me to help her, but I oblige every time.

"Thank you, darling," she says.

Grabbing her sheers, she places the flowers on the counter, neatly separating them. One by one, she carefully trims the stems and removes any extra leaves before arranging them beautifully in a vase. Growing up, I was always impressed by her floral skills. She could have easily opened a shop but stayed home and cared for me and my father.

"Anything for you. How's your day been so far? Anything interesting going on in your life?"

"Son, it's been peaceful. I woke up, did my morning prayer, and then walked with some of the ladies in the neighborhood. Now I have you here with me. Could it get any better?"

"I know I'm the best part of your day, but I think it can improve." I wink at her.

"You're proposing?" She turns and faces me, eyes wider than her smile.

"Not exactly." I laugh.

"Then what is it, child?" She places her hands on her hips. "Don't keep an old lady guessing. It's rude, and I know I've raised you better than that."

"I'm going to be a father."

"Say it ain't so?" My mom throws her hands in the air and does a little shuffle.

"That's you're happy dance, right?" I slightly laugh.

"Boy, come give me a hug." She smiles.

<u>2</u>

Happy 4 U

Monday, October 18, 2010

Skye

"Were we not on the same page?" I shout through the phone. "I told you not to tell anyone. That *included* your mom."

"It's not that big of a deal. It's just my mom. What's the problem?"

"I love your mom, but the problem is I wasn't ready for anyone to know, Lance."

After returning home from my doctor's appointment, Mrs. Evans greeted me with congratulatory messages and plans. I knew when he told her she'd be ready to plan a baby shower. She has a good heart, and I'm not trying to be the person that breaks it.

To be quite frank, I'm not entirely sure I'm ready to become a mom, but it seems as though that decision may have already been made for me. If I choose to terminate this pregnancy, Lance will undoubtedly hate me, and his mother will be devastated. If I refuse to bring this baby to full term, I will be seen as the villain in their fairytale story.

Perhaps I should have kept this information to myself to avoid the overwhelming opinions of others. My thoughts are already clouded enough. There's no more space for anyone else's.

Nonetheless, here I am, struggling with what seems to be the biggest decision of my life. More significant than the day I told my mother I was never moving back home. Man was she pissed. I thought she would have been happy not to put up with me not meeting *her* expectations. She didn't hesitate to tell me I was making the biggest mistake of my life.

I had a clear plan during college: study business, intern at my father's law firm, and eventually attend law school. I didn't quite end up going down that route.

My perspective shifted as I took on side jobs to earn extra cash. I enjoyed the freedom of working on website creation, editing, and ghostwriting projects. It was a refreshing change of pace, and my mind wasn't consumed with thoughts of all the ways I'd be a disappointment. I was finally living for myself.

Ultimately, I pursued that creative career path to avoid moving back in with my parents. My father was proud of me for choosing to do what I loved and not what I thought he wanted me to do, but that mother of mine couldn't help but belittle me and tell me how other graduates would have been grateful for the opportunity to have a secure job and place to live.

"I'm sorry, baby, but this is the best news we've had since my dad's passing. I had to tell her," he responds, hoping to calm me down.

"There you go, trying to make me feel bad. All you had to do was wait three months, and you couldn't even do that."

"First off, I'm not trying to make you feel bad. I'm just saying."

I can feel myself getting upset. My eyes are getting heavy, and if I stay on the phone with him any longer, I'm going to start crying. "Let's talk about this later before I say something I'll regret."

"I love you—"

I hang up the phone before Lance can complete his sentence. *Why does he do that?* I question as I throw my phone on the bed.

Whenever he does something I dislike or have repeatedly asked him not to, he brings up his dad's passing. I'm not sure if he did it purposely or not, but all he had to do was respect my wishes.

Initially, I empathized with his situation. I have both my parents and couldn't fathom losing them suddenly, despite how rude my mother may be, so I tended to stay off his back when it came to minor situations, but this isn't minor to me.

Sitting on the bed, I pick up my phone to call Emily and notice a few messages—the first from Lance. I'm sure I hurt his feelings, hanging up with no real goodbye or a simple "I love you too."

Lance: *Sorry, babe, I didn't mean to upset you. I love you!*

I keep my thoughts to myself and refrain from telling him what's on my mind. I'm sure he'll come over as soon as he finishes work. I can't imagine him being able to focus on anything else until he knows we're on the same page. I plan on sending him a sweet message in a little to help ease his worry.

Going back to my messages, I catch a glimpse of Desmond's name. I immediately close out my text and start pacing back and forth. *What does he want?* Desmond hasn't bothered contacting me since our breakup, which was understandable. I wouldn't have reached out to him if the shoe was on the other foot. He deserved an explanation for my choice, and I didn't bother giving him one out of selfishness.

Picking up my phone, I dial Emily, and she answers on the first ring. "How was your doctor's appointment?" She asks before I say, "Hello."

"It was good or whatever," I rush my response. "Desmond texted me."

We both sit on the phone in silence for what seems like an eternity, but it's only thirty seconds—thirty long seconds.

"Did you hear me?"

"Yes, I heard you. I'm just…surprised," Emily finally finds the words. "Well, what did it say?"

"I haven't read it. I called you as soon as I saw his name."

"What the fuck are you waiting for? Look at the damn text."

"Em," I pause, "I'm scared. It's been close to a year. What could he possibly have to say to me after all this time? He probably wants to kill me after seeing me in that damn store."

"We won't know until you look at the text message. So, look at the damn text," Emily screams.

"Okay, I'm going to put you on speaker."

Going into my messages, the first words I see are: *Are you happy?*

Not exactly.

Seeing those words next to his name and our picture made me sad. I can't believe I never changed his caller ID photo. *Why didn't I delete his contact completely?* Lance wouldn't be happy to see a picture of me kissing another man on the cheek pop up on my phone.

I should probably change that.

"Well," Emily clears her throat.

"I'm opening it now."

The first message reads:

Desmond: *Should I be telling you congrats? I know you wouldn't be buying all those tests if you weren't sure you were pregnant. I'm happy 4 U!*

"And he put the number four with the letter U," I inform her.

"He's happy for you? That's a crock of shit. He didn't even bother spelling out the words," Emily snarls. "That man couldn't be happy for you if he wanted to. He's dying without you by his side."

"What makes you so sure about that?" I question.

"First of all, he hasn't dated anyone since you broke up with the poor guy, and he was just over Jordan's house basically crying about how he didn't think your relationship would cease to exist, but don't tell him I told you that."

He does miss me! Well, obviously, Skye. You spent almost every day in each other's presence for four years. That's one thousand four hundred sixty days.

"I probably won't even text back," I tell Emily. "There's nothing for us to discuss."

"Sure you won't," she says sarcastically. "Is that all he said?"

"Yeah, that's all," I lie.

<u>10</u>

The Change

Friday, April 3, 2009

Skye

The bleeding isn't stopping—I don't know what to do. I sat in the bathroom, trying not to think the worst, but as I wiped and stared at the blood on the tissue, I became terrified. I know this can't be normal. It's entirely too much.

Desmond won't answer the phone. I've called repeatedly, and now it's going straight to voicemail. I don't know if it's dead or if he's ignoring me, but I'm pissed off and scared. I'm home by myself with no one to lean on. This isn't supposed to be happening.

I don't want this to be happening.

We had one more week, and I would get to tell everyone about our baby—our beautiful blessing made out of pure love. Desmond was right there with me as I took the test, handing me the stick and counting the minutes until I could see the results. I knew I was pregnant the second I looked at him. His eyes lit up. We were the happiest we'd ever been. Everything was following into place. The only thing missing was an engagement ring.

For our pregnancy announcement, we planned everything out. We would gather with our closest friends and some of my family members. Toward the end of the night, before everyone got too carried away, we'd play a game revealing we'd be parents. Desmond couldn't wait for the day to come.

What did I do wrong? I must have done something wrong. I fall to the floor in tears.

With no one else to call, I pick up my phone to call 911. "Something is happening. I, I think I hurt my baby." I cry to the dispatcher. "It hurts so bad, and the bleeding… won't stop. Something isn't right!"

I lay across the bathroom floor, trying to minimize the pain. It feels like my uterus is being pulled apart. I can't believe I'm going through this alone—going through this at all. It's not like I can call my parents. They live hours away and don't even know I'm pregnant. Desmond's parents passed away when he was a teen, so they aren't an option either. I could call Emily, but one, she has no idea I'm pregnant, and two, she'd freak the hell out. I don't need her theatrics. I need a calming voice and hand beside me—him.

"Ma'am, is there a child with you?" The dispatcher asks.

"No, no. I'm pregnant," I confirm.

"How far along are you?"

"Three months." I cry harder, holding onto my stomach. I was beginning to show.

"Ma'am, are you able to drive, or is there someone who can drive you to the hospital? It's important for you to get examined," The dispatcher asks calmly. I'm appreciative of her soothing voice. It's the only thing getting me through this nightmare.

"I don't think so. Please send someone. I don't want to lose my baby," I weep.

As we make our way to the emergency department, I can only think about how quickly my blessing is being taken away from me. I don't need a doctor to confirm what I already know. I felt it—I felt life draining from me on my bathroom floor, and the man I loved couldn't be reached. I know it's not like he could have stopped my body from reacting, but he could have at least been there to calm me down—get me to the hospital faster. Instead, I lay there in my blood, doing everything in my power to keep our baby with me, but I'm sure my prayers weren't answered.

After hours of waiting, a doctor is able to check on me. The nurse takes my blood, and the doctor does an ultrasound to confirm what I know—I was miscarrying. I'm given options—finish miscarrying naturally, take medication, or have a D&C procedure. The procedure wouldn't take more than twenty minutes, but I opt against it because I want to be in the comfort of my home. I need to do this in my safe space. Once the doctor gives me instructions on how to use the

medicine, I take a cab home. A fucking cab.
If I don't stop bleeding after two weeks, I
have to come back.

I have never felt so alone.

~

Monday, April 20, 2009

I thought it best to take some time for
myself.

I cleared my calendar and informed my
clients I'd need to take off due to a family
emergency. They didn't need to know the
real reason for my absence. I'd work twice
as hard once I was cleared to work again.
Once I felt like it, honestly.

My bed has been my best friend,
therapist, and companion for weeks. Here,
I've been taking the time to heal—crying
nonstop.

I wasn't aware I could grieve a life that
hadn't even entered the world. Dealing
with the realization that motherhood has
been stripped from me is the worst pain,
physical and mental. I never imagined

something like this would happen to us. I expected a smooth pregnancy, especially since my mother always bragged about me doing all the work for her.

"You practically birthed yourself," she would say. "You've been trying to get away from me since birth."

Ha, she even made my entering into the world about me not wanting to be around her. That mother of mine is something.

Thoughts of losing my child before getting the chance to meet them never crossed my mind. I thought it was impossible.

I struggled to accept the news I had received at the hospital, and Desmond was doing his best to support me. However, I couldn't help but resent him for not being there that night. That was the night he decided to go out with his friends, get drunk, and not come home while I was facing the most harrowing moment of my life.

I was counting on him to be there for me, but he wasn't. I felt so alone and helpless. I couldn't turn to anyone. It was hard enough dealing with the physical pain of losing something so precious, but the emotional pain was even worse. I felt like I had failed, and I was filled with anger.

He tried to reassure me that we could try again, that my dreams of having a family with him weren't over, but it felt like it. The final traces of the little person that was growing inside me had vanished entirely from my body a few days ago. My doctor confirmed it. It changed everything.

We weren't the same anymore.

"Are you just going to stay locked up in this room?" Desmond pokes his head through the door. "Let's go for a walk around the neighborhood or something."

"Does it look like I'm up for walking?"

"You gotta do something. Get up and walk for ten minutes at least," he insists.

"And see all the moms in the neighborhood strolling their babies around?"

"Skye, I didn't mean—"

"Let me be. I'll come out when I'm ready. Go be with your friends or something."

"Is this how things are going to be? Me trying to be there for you, and you pushing me away." He steps into the room.

"Please just go."

"Skye, why won't you let me be here for you? All I want to do is be here for you. I want to help you through this."

"I don't want you to. I don't want you here." I throw our baby's teddy bear at the door and put the covers over my head.

I don't come back out until I hear him walking away and the front door closing behind him. It's so hard for me to look at him. To pretend I'm okay. I'm not.

<u>11</u>

Long Shot

Wednesday, November 10, 2010

Desmond

It's been about a month since I saw Skye, and she's been on my mind more than before. No matter how hard I try, memories of her flood my brain. I know it's unhealthy to dwell on the past, but I can't help it when she was supposed to be my future. I can't move on from that, even if she has.

Whenever I see something that reminds me of her, my heart sinks. When I leave my apartment for my morning runs, I think back to when I bought us bikes, and she was terrified to get on, thinking she'd forgotten how to ride. When I go to the mall and walk past the food court, I think about how we'd stop at the Korean stand to get rice and teriyaki chicken that she'd smother in sriracha. Every chance we got, she'd talk me into going to the mall to have that same meal.

I miss her.

It's been nine months since our last real conversation, and I said some things I can't take back. Words I didn't mean. There's a new guy in her life, and I don't need him to think I'm trying to overstep. No one has time to be fighting over a woman. *My woman.* Until I get that title back, I'll continue playing my role as the longing ex-boyfriend.

I figured I'd congratulate her on becoming a mother to make the situation less awkward, but she never responded. That didn't go as I had planned. I'm sure she wants nothing to do with me, but I want everything to do with her, baby or not.

The truth is, I want to reconnect with Skye and make sure she's truly happy with her decision to start a family with someone else. There was a time when it was supposed to be us building a life together—family. Instead, I let our relationship fall apart and had to deal with the aftermath of it all. It eats away at me more than I admit to anyone, to myself.

I regret the day I left her lonely—without a simple message telling her my phone was dying. If I had been home, maybe we could have prevented the miscarriage. I could have gotten her to the hospital when her body started a fight she couldn't win. Doctors told her she couldn't have done anything to stop it, but you can't help but question God's plan. Wonder why he thought you and your lady weren't fit to bring a child into the world. Was it not meant to be?

I envisioned a beautiful baby girl with eyes that light up the night like the moon— the same as her mother's—big and bright. Eyes I dreamed of looking into and getting the chance to experience love at first sight all over again.

Reality hurts, and as much as I try to erase the unfortunate outcome from my mind, I can't.

"Here goes nothing," I say as I pull out my phone to text Skye, hoping she responds this time around.

If I'm left alone at the restaurant where I officially asked her to be mine, it's going to be humiliating—a black man dressed in a tux with flowers and no date. I'd laugh if I saw it, but that's a sad and embarrassing sight.

I don't think Skye would do me like that. Crush a man's heart after stomping it out already. That would be some cold-hearted shit. Nah, she definitely wouldn't do that. I never thought she'd end things with me, so anything is possible.

I could have fought harder for us, especially when she needed me most, but a man's pride can also be one's downfall. Getting her to meet me at our restaurant is a long shot, but I'm willing to try. Having her back in my life would mean everything to me...even if it's simply as friends.

<u>12</u>

Contemplating

Friday, November 12, 2010

Skye

What does he expect from me?

We haven't had a genuine conversation since I left him at his door to wonder where we went wrong. I was never supposed to see him again after that. I thought I'd accepted the reality of us existing as if we were never a couple. I was doing fine without him. I was moving on, building a new life with a new man, but Desmond had me contemplating it all.

I have less than 24 hours to decide whether or not I'll show my face at the restaurant where we sat down wide-eyed and giggly, creating some of our earliest memories.

I'd usually reach out to Emily when in need of someone who'll talk me out of making the wrong decision, but for this, I can't. Emily believes Desmond is my end-all-be-all. She is a diehard Desmond fan. She will get overly excited and assume I'm getting rid of Lance so I can run back into his arms, but that can't happen.

My life is moving in a new direction.

I'm continuing the pregnancy, and I refuse to do it alone. Single mother isn't a title I'm comfortable having. After all, I had my perception of what a traditional family should be like.

After my outburst, I eventually told Lance about my miscarriage with Desmond. How it turned me into a broken woman, fearful of attempting to bring life into the world again. I planned on taking that information to my grave. That unfortunate event is one I try hard to forget, but I'm reminded more and more of it as the days go by. The thought always brings me back to the second I sat down to pee—the blood-stained tissue and underwear. Everything about it hurts to this day, but since I'm carrying Lance's child, I needed to explain why his revealing my pregnancy to his mother was upsetting.

I also had to get honest with myself. The possible outcomes of what could take place. *What if I did decide to get rid of my baby?* It could be a serious mistake. There could be the chance of me never being able to conceive again. I can't give up on becoming a mother, one more loving, supportive, and attentive than the mother I was given. If I were to go through with an abortion, I'd potentially eliminate the chance of motherhood for good.

> **Desmond:** *I'm not sure if you can make it since I haven't heard from you, but I want you to know I'll be at the restaurant at seven o'clock on the dot. I've requested our table in the back. Hope to see you there.*

"He thinks he's slick," I accidentally blurt out.

"Who?" Lance yells from the living room.

Fuck.

I completely forgot he didn't go to work tonight. He's been in the living room so focused on that damn game I forgot he was even here.

"Just some asshole on this reality show I'm watching." I lie and quickly turn my TV to an episode of Love & HipHop. I'd hate for him to walk into this room only to see me with the television off and phone in hand, smirking at a text from my ex. He says I've been acting off these days, so I've been doing my best to get my shit in line.

"What reality show got you all riled up like that?"

"Love & HipHop," I respond.

"I didn't even know you still watched that bullshit." I could hear his voice getting closer to the room.

"I usually don't, but I'm bored," I say, quickly deleting Desmond's message and setting the phone under my pillow. I haven't told Lance my ex has been reaching out to me. I don't want to worry him. Lance will be at work tomorrow, so Desmond's timing is perfect. I can see what he needs to say and return home without ever having to tell a soul I met up with him.

"Why don't you come in the living room with me? We can cuddle under the covers with snacks and watch a movie."

"How's your game going to feel about you abandoning her," I joke. I swear that man treats his PlayStation like his side chick. I'm not sure if it gets more attention or me. I might be the side chick as much as he plays on that shit.

"This PlayStation isn't carrying my legacy," he says, rubbing my still, very flat stomach.

"Why must you do that?" My eyes shift to his hand and then back up to him. "Can't you wait until I'm at least showing?"

"It's just that I'm excited to become a dad. I wish mine were here to witness it."

"Me too, but guess what?" I take his hand.

"What?"

"At least we'll always have someone looking over our baby. A guardian angel," I say, grabbing him by the face and kissing him with every bit of passion.

Lance makes me a tad less terrified about becoming a mom, and his kisses are reassuring.

"You sure you still want to watch that movie?" I ask, pulling away from him.

"Yes, but first, I want to watch the faces you make when I put this dick in you."

He is so nasty!

<u>13</u>

Rain Check

Saturday, November 13, 2010

Skye

Today is the day. I've officially decided to meet up with Desmond. I feel less anxious than yesterday. I have to give Lance all the credit for that. How he tended to my body last night was enough to stop my mind from overthinking Desmond and me.

He has a gift for instilling a sense of invincibility in me and making me feel like we could overcome any obstacle. He makes me feel like no one can tear us apart whenever he lays my body down. This morning, he practically had to rip me from his neck. I didn't want him to leave my side, and he probably wouldn't have if he had some clean clothes here. If I had it my way, I'd stay in bed with him all day, getting my back blown out. Unfortunately, we don't have that luxury. Rather than spending a lovely Saturday together, he needs to rest up for work while I prepare for dinner with Desmond—a dinner I should be telling him about but won't.

When Lance leaves, I dash to my closet and frantically search for the perfect outfit. I want to look amazing but not too amazing. I want Desmond to be blown away by my beauty and realize that he made a huge mistake by letting me go.

Technically, I let him go, but he should have fought harder to keep me.

As I scanned my clothes, I couldn't find anything that fit the bill. It's like my wardrobe is conspiring against me!

"It's a sign, Skye. Don't fucking go," I say, throwing another pair of jeans to the side. As I continue throwing clothing items around, my phone goes off.

Desmond: *Looking forward to seeing you tonight.*

"Sign number two. God is definitely telling me to go. I need to give the man the closure he deserves, and I have to look good doing it," I say to myself. It looks like me and Emily need to hit up the mall. She's always down for a shopping trip.

Skye: *Are you busy?*

Emily: *Why?*

Skye: *Can I not check in on a friend to see if she wants to spend her savings in the mall?*

Emily: *Sorry. You know I love a good sale. Be there in 40?*

Skye: *You read my mind. See you soon and whatever that attitude was, drop it quick. We both can't be moody bitches.*

I wonder what her problem is.

Heading into the bathroom, I quickly strip off the pajamas I'd lounged in all morning and turn on the shower. The warm water feels soothing against my skin, and it's helping ease my worries regarding tonight. The gentle scent of vanilla fills the air as I lather up. Rinsing off, I wrap myself in my favorite fluffy towel. I hide them whenever Lance comes over. I got these made specially for me. They're expensive and not meant to be used by anyone other than me.

Going to my closet, I settle on a simple but flattering outfit—a pair of skinny jeans, a flowy blouse, and ankle boots. I run a brush through my hair and swipe on a bit of mascara just as Emily calls my phone to let me know she's waiting out front. I grab my purse and head out the door.

~

"What are you and Jordan doing tonight?" I ask Emily to gauge if she has any idea about my plans for the night. It's not like she'll judge me, but I'm not in the sharing mood. Maybe I'll fill her in once the dinner is over.

"We usually have a date night, but I'm considering staying inside tonight. I need time to unwind. Between my staff and my fight with Jordan, I'm exhausted."

"You and Jordan…fighting? I can't even see it. The most I've seen you two argue over is where to eat." I laugh.

"Well, this time, it's serious," Emily responds.

"Like life or death serious?"

"More like if he doesn't propose to me in the next six months, I'm fucking leaving him," Emily shouts, forgetting we're in a tiny ass store full of people.

"When did you decide this?"

It was out of character for Emily to issue ultimatums, especially regarding her relationship with Jordan. I always thought they were perfect for each other. They'd been together for eight years, which is no small feat, but they were still young— Emily, 25, and Jordan, 26. I could sympathize with him if he weren't ready to take the giant leap into marriage. *Was a man that young ever ready?*

"It's been eight years, Skye. How much more time does he need to decide if he wants to marry me?" Emily asks, rampaging through the clothing rack.

"You know he wants to marry you," I reassure her, pulling her into me.

"Then why hasn't he proposed yet?" Emily begins to cry.

As I look over at Emily and then around at the curious onlookers, my heart goes out to her. My girl is an emotional being in nature, but never has she broken out in tears in a public setting. She holds that shit in until she's around people she feels safest. There's no way I can bring myself to go meet up with Desmond while she's like this. We consider this a "Girlfriend 911." We drop everything and everyone when one of us is in need, and she needs me. I send Desmond a quick text and get my girl out of here.

Once I get Emily to the car, I drive without a destination. I'm not in the mood to sit in my apartment—the bar is out of the question since I can't drink, and there is no way we can sit at a restaurant the way she's crying uncontrollably. A quiet car ride will have to do until I figure something out.

As we drove down the freeway and listened to R&B, Emily eventually fell asleep, tears streaming down her face. I try to wrap my head around her situation. It's common knowledge that Emily and Jordan will undoubtedly be married. She's been saying he's going to be her husband since we were seventeen. That's a long ass time. It's longer than any relationship I've ever been in. During those eight years, he's made it clear that he only has eyes for Emily. He won't even glance at another woman. He barely speaks to them. *Why is Emily giving him an ultimatum?* It all seems a bit extreme to me.

After driving for an hour, we end up at the beach. It's almost as if destiny led us here, knowing we both could use the calming sounds of the ocean waves—allowing us to find inner peace—and confront the struggles we're quietly battling.

Looking at Emily, still asleep, I let her rest for a bit longer. Walking across the street to the small convenience store, I get her a canned wine, candy, chips, and myself a peach tea. Once I'm back at the car, I pop the trunk to remove the extra blankets I keep. I find a spot nearby and lay them out on the sand with our goodies.

"Emily, wake up," I say, nudging her, "We're here."

"Where is *here?*" She asks, squinting her eyes.

"Some place beautiful and relaxing. A place that will take your mind off of whatever worries you. Come on," I say, linking my arm with hers and pulling her out of the car. "It's time for a little therapy."

"How long was I sleep for?"

"Forty minutes or so. I didn't want to wake you and wasn't sure what you wanted to do, so I kept driving."

"Well, this is perfect. Sorry if I ruined any of your plans for the day," Emily says, sitting on the blanket.

"Don't be sorry. I didn't have anything going on," I lie. "Even if I did, you're my priority. Just let me know how you want this to go. We can sit here silently, talk about what's happening with you and J, or dance around on this empty beach like two crazy women. Take your pick."

"How about we do them all?"

"I got you," I say, pulling out my phone to put on some Sade.

"I got you something," I announce, handing Emily the canned wine. "It's not that fancy stuff you like, but It'll have to do."

"I'd drink anything right about now," she says, on the verge of tears again.

"Em, are you okay?" I ask, moving closer to her.

"Yes, no… I don't know." She starts balling again. "I might have breast cancer."

I didn't know how to respond. *Breast cancer? How? When? Why?* She never mentioned anything being wrong with her. If I think the worst, I can only imagine her thought process. It's a scary and uncomfortable situation to be in. As much as I want to freak out, I know I need to remain calm for Emily. If she sees me about to lose my shit, she'll have a complete meltdown *again*.

"Emily, are you sure? Have you been looked at yet?"

"Well...no. I thought I felt something when I was in the shower a few days ago. I'm scared. What if I'm fucking dying? I'm unmarried and haven't even had the chance to start my family," Emily weeps.

"Emily," I say, taking hold of her hand, "It may not be anything. You have to try to relax. Don't overthink anything just yet. Not until you get some solid answers."

"How can I not freak out? I think there's a lump in my chest. We all know that means I'm going to have to cut off my tits. My beautiful ass tits, Skye," she yells, squeezing the life out of them.

I release a gut-wrenching laugh, and I'm so happy no one but Emily is around to hear it. I shouldn't even be laughing right now, but I couldn't hold it in after that. I didn't even get the chance to. Breast cancer is serious, but I need her to make an appointment at least and not jump to conclusions. She's already convinced herself she's dying and willing to end her relationship over it.

"This isn't funny, Skye. I could die, and my boyfriend doesn't want to marry me."

"You're right. You're right. It's not funny, but trust me when I say you're wrong about Jordan not wanting to marry you. The man worships you, and you shouldn't want to get married just because you think you'll magically drop dead in the next six months. That's not fair to him."

I feel like I defend this man as much as she defends Desmond. I guess we know a good man when we see one.

"But what about what I want?"

"Emily, he's been giving you everything you've wanted for as long as I've known him. You need to explain to him why you freaked out and apologize. Then you need to schedule an exam so we can figure out if we have a serious situation on our hands. We'll figure out the rest from there."

In the middle of our conversation, Emily's phone goes off. It's Jordan. I watch as she listens to him quietly. Just that quick a smile graces her beautiful face.

"What did he say?" I ask the minute she puts the phone away.

"He'll drop everything and marry me today." She lights up. That was all she needed to hear.

"Told you so."

"Get me back home to my man." She jumps up.

"So, our time together means nothing," I whine. "You're just going to use me up and leave me hanging."

"It meant everything," she says, pulling me into a reassuring hug. "Thank you for always being there for me. I will make the appointment tomorrow."

"Promise?"

"Pinky promise." She extends her pinky.

"Alright then. I guess I'm okay with returning you to Prince Charming."

<u>14</u>

Get Out Your Feelings

Saturday, November 13, 2010

Desmond

Damn, I was hella excited about spending some time with Skye tonight. I guess that shit wasn't meant to be. It feels good knowing she was going to show up, though. I swore she was going to leave me hanging.

Maybe that means she'll let me take her out another day.

I want to know what's happening in her life beyond the baby growing inside her. Is she happy? Is her family doing well? Are her parents still healthy and wealthy? I want to know how her business is doing—if she's written any stories of her own instead of letting others use her words. Skye is talented in many ways.

I miss watching her sitting crossed leg on my big bean bag that she swore she hated, laser-focused on whatever task she had taken on, whether that be building a website from scratch, revamping someone's existing site, or working on a story. I miss my friend. Skye was more than just some girl I fell in love with on sight—she was my best friend.

When I received her "Girlfriend 911" text, I was a little disappointed, but I knew it meant something was going on with Emily. They'd been using it far longer than I'd known the two of them. It's how I first learned about Skye back in college. I had never seen her untangle herself from Jordan's embrace that fast until one of those texts came through. He knew exactly what it meant.

Speaking of, I need to call his ass.

I grab my phone and dial his number to see if everything is good. "Aye, what you getting into today?" I ask as soon as he answers.

"I was supposed to be taking Emily out tonight, but she's not talking to me."

"What you do?" I ask out of curiosity.

"Why it gotta be something I did? Why can't it be her?"

"I'm not blaming anyone here, but Emily doesn't get upset. You did something."

"You at the house?" Jordan asks.

"Yup. My plans fell through."

I didn't tell him I was supposed to meet with Skye. Nigga would have had a million questions for me. Then he would have told Emily, and she would have tried to crash our date, or whatever it was supposed to be.

"Nigga when do you ever actually have *real* plans. You don't be doing shit."

"Ha-ha, shut the fuck up. You don't know my life."

Jordan was right, though. If I'm not working out, at the gym training people, hosting a boot camp, or eating somewhere, I'm usually not doing a damn thing.

"Yeah, okay," he chuckles, "I'm about to be on my way."

"Coo."

Jordan came through with several bottles, and I could see he was upset. I've been friends with Jordan for as long as I've known Emily, and he's always been careful to avoid drama with her—always gentle in how he expresses his feelings. Even a slight change in his tone could bring on the waterworks.

"Did Skye ever try to force marriage on you?"

"Not really. We used to talk about it a lot, though."

"But did she ever threaten to leave you over it?"

"Never. When it came to marriage, we were always on the same page. We both knew we wanted to be married, but we didn't put a date on it."

"Man, I wish Emily would get off my case about it, but now she's giving me no choice," Jordan says, pouring a shot. "I'm still young. I figured we still had about five years before having to walk down the aisle, and now she's giving me six months, or she out."

"Like breaking up with you, out?"

"Nigga, yes. She is really on one," Jordan says, shaking his head.

"What you gon' do?"

"I can stand my ground and risk losing my girl, or I can go out and buy a ring."

"Man, that's a tough one," I say, walking toward the kitchen to grab a beer from the fridge. I'm not really in the mood to have anything strong, especially with this man over here complaining about marrying a woman he wants to spend the rest of his life with.

"The real question you should ask yourself is, can you live without her? Could you see yourself starting over with someone new?"

"These bitches don't have anything that I want. I'm good where I'm at," he assures me.

"Then what's the fucking problem? It sounds like you're just difficult. I know you don't want to end up like me...out here dry. The woman I love is building a life with another nigga, and I'm just stuck. You don't even want to know the kind of pain I'm feeling."

"You know it's not too late," he informs me. "I don't know why the two of you are playing this long-ass game with each other when it's obvious y'all miss each other."

"Did she say that?"

"She ain't have to say it. It's been implied."

"Implying it and saying it are two different things, but this ain't even about me and her," I say, trying to avoid further conversation about Skye. We're talking about his shit. "Get out your feelings and man the fuck up before you don't have no woman to go home to at all."

<u>15</u>

The Link Up

Saturday, November 13, 2010
Skye

Skye: *Can you come over?*

Sending a, *come and see me,* text to my ex was probably not the most brilliant move to make, but after spending time with Emily, I couldn't resist. I wanted to hear him out. I wanted to see his face. I was supposed to be seeing him tonight anyway. It's too late to make the reservation he set up, and I have a hunch he already canceled it after receiving my 911 message. Plus, I probably shouldn't be seen with him in public.

Rumor spreads fast.

Sitting on the couch anxiously awaiting Desmond's response, I second-guess myself.

"Why are you so stupid, Skye? I could tell him I'm tired, and we can meet another day. But I already canceled once. It would be odd if I canceled again." I'm talking to myself as I pace around my apartment nervously—wringing my hands, trying to shake off the guilt gnawing at me.

Twenty minutes pass, and I hear a knock at the door.

"Oh shit, is that him?" I cover my mouth.

Putting my eye on the peephole, I see Desmond standing there in all his glory. He's holding a pizza box in one hand and a DVD in the other.

I wonder what movie he brought.

I run to the standing mirror sitting in my living room to make sure I don't look a complete mess.

"One second," I yell as he rings the doorbell.

Fixing my ponytail in the mirror, I realize I'm wearing only a T-shirt. It would have been okay once upon a time, but now, not so much. I run to my room to throw on some joggers and a hoodie. At the last minute, I turn around to apply some gloss to my lips. *Just because he's my ex doesn't mean I have to downplay my features.* Excited, I race back to the living room and open the door.

"Took you long enough," he says, smiling that smile I love.

I don't realize I'm staring at him like a lost child until he says, "Are you going to invite me in?"

"S-s-sorry," I stutter, moving to the side so he can enter.

He's a sight to see.

"Don't be nervous. I'm not going to bite." He smirks as he walks past me. "Where should I put the pizza."

"The table in the living room is fine. Looks like we'll be watching a movie."

I'm barely holding onto my composure, every fiber in my being yearning to break free and show him the full display of my pearly whites. Being in his presence has got me feeling giddy as fuck. I should be ashamed.

"I figured pizza and a movie would make up for the date we had to cancel."

"It wasn't a date." I snap out of my dream world. He shakes his head and chuckles as I stand in awkward silence.

"Um, so, Did Jordan come to see you?" I break my trance.

"Yes. Talked some sense into that fool, and then he went on his merry way."

"You can have a seat, and I'll grab some plates. Would you like water or something?"

"Whatever is fine," he says, setting up the movie before sitting on the couch. I'm surprised how comfortable he is around me. It's as if nothing happened between us. We've always had a natural vibe with one another, but here I go, being all awkward.

Of course, he wants something to drink. Who the fuck eats pizza and doesn't wash it down with something? I was with the man for four years, for goodness' sake. Get it together girl.

Walking back into the living room, I place the paper plates on the table along with napkins and sit a beer in front of Desmond. I vividly remember how much he enjoyed pairing his pizza with one. It always puzzled me why I consistently kept my fridge stocked with them. I wasn't a fan, and Lance rarely drank them when he came over. Perhaps subconsciously, I bought them hoping to have a moment like tonight.

"Aww, you remembered."

"Stuff like that is pretty hard to forget." I grin.

As I grab a slice, our hands abruptly touch. The sensation is electrifying—thrilling, but at the same time, it makes me tense up. Our spark hasn't died out, and though I should be pulling away, I don't think I want to.

"My bad," Desmond says, being the first to move his hand.

"Here you go." I place a few slices on his plate.

"Thank you." He smirks at me and then leans back into the couch. I watch him as he takes a bite. "Ready for me to press play?" He laughs after catching my gaze.

Shyly, I look away, trying to gather myself. "Um, yeah. What are we watching?"

"Twilight Eclipse. I hope you haven't seen it yet."

"You'll be happy to hear that I haven't."

"Neither have I," he replies.

My cheeks were ablaze with heat, and I couldn't hide my smile anymore. Desmond knew me inside out, like a beloved book he'd read a hundred times. It would only confirm his suspicions if I tried to glance away now. My heart was racing, and I needed it to slow down before it burst out of my chest. I shouldn't have been this excited, but the realization that we had both denied ourselves the guilty pleasure of watching the latest vampire flick from our favorite franchise had me beaming. We planned to catch the movie together on the big screen, but I had to go and ruin everything by starting a new relationship.

As I sit beside him, a rush of memories floods my mind—days we'd decide to avoid the football games and frat parties so we could spend quality time away from the crowds. We'd walk to the local pizza shop next to campus, grab snacks from the 7-

Eleven across the street, and then walk to his apartment around the corner to watch movies all night. I always preferred his apartment over my dorm because we could avoid the heart-eyes and whispers from my roommates.

I want to snuggle up to him like we did in the early stages of our dating—to feel his warmth, but I hesitate. I settle for the safety of my throw blanket, creating a comfortable barrier between us with one of the extra decorative pillows sitting on my couch.

"Ew, she's bold," I shout as I watch Bella slice open her arm to save Edward from being ripped apart by Victoria and Riley. The lengths this girl has gone to stay by this Vampire's side. He's not even that attractive, but I'm here for their commitment to one another.

"You wouldn't do that to save the love of your life?" Desmond asks, looking over at me.

"Good thing we'll never have to find out unless you're a vampire or something."

The silence between us is loud. I didn't mean to say that, but the words came naturally. I didn't even think before speaking.

Desmond glances at me—reading me with his eyes before he speaks. "If I were, I'd risk my life a thousand times to ensure you're safe."

~

Slowly opening my eyes, I can sense his arm around me—his hand slightly above my ass but close enough for my mind to wonder. My head is resting on his shoulder, and I know it shouldn't be there, but my body is too weak to move from this couch, nor does it want to. I'm relaxed where I am, and I want to hold on to this because soon, I'll have to get back to reality. Living in the past won't do us any good.

I can see the sun is beginning to rise, which means we fell asleep. I recall stopping my lips from meeting his after he told me he'd do anything to protect me.

Those words would have brought me to my knees had I been standing. Maybe it was my hormones, or perhaps the part of me that missed him. All I know is I wanted him.

Typically, nights like last night would have ended with my legs wrapped around his waist and him leading me to the bedroom. Since I'm another man's woman and carrying that man's child, I shouldn't have even thought it possible.

What could he possibly want from his pregnant ex-girlfriend anyway? I probably turned him off if he still found me slightly attractive.

Tilting my head slightly, I watch Desmond resting. I do my best to stay firm in my position so he doesn't wake up, remembering that the slightest motion would awake him from his slumber.

"Good morning, pretty lady," he says, kissing my forehead.

Too late, I think as I sit up.

"Sorry, I didn't mean to wake you."

"It's fine, you know I can't sleep for long. If I slept any longer, my arm might have fallen off."

"Oh shit, I am so sorry," I say, leaning forward. "Was that wrapped around me all night?"

"Yes, but I didn't mind." He smiles.

Maybe I didn't turn him off.

"Um, do you want me to make you breakfast?" I ask, wanting him to stay longer.

"I'd hate to take up too much more of your time, but I'd love to stay. Is that good with you?" I nod, and he says," What about coffee and a bagel? I know you can't cook."

"Oh, shut up." I laugh. "You're in luck, though. I have both, but first, let me brush my teeth," I say, covering my mouth.

"Glad I didn't have to say it," he says, plugging his nose. "Do you have an extra toothbrush?"

"You're one to talk. Follow me."

As we get up, I see Desmond looking around for anything indicating that Lance is living with me, but there's nothing. That's the one area of our lives we didn't rush into.

"You have a nice place," he says as we enter my room.

"Trust me, it did not look this nice before. I eventually set up all my furniture and decor about three months ago."

"What took you so long?"

"I didn't know if I would be staying here permanently," I answer, passing Desmond a toothbrush from the drawer where I keep extra bathroom essentials.

"Oh," he says, slowly taking it from my hand. "Well, it looks nice."

"Thank you!"

Turning on the water, I reach for the toothpaste, and our hands touch again. *More sparks.*

"Let me," he says, taking it from me, applying it to mine and then his.

"A gentleman, even in the morning."

"But you knew that already." He smirks and proceeds to brush his teeth.

"Nice and fresh." I grin in the mirror once I'm done.

"Great, 'cause that shit was funky," Desmond says, throwing the toothbrush in the garbage and walking back toward the kitchen.

"Oh wow, you have some nerve," I yell behind him. "Yours wasn't too welcoming either."

Staying behind, I use the bathroom and try to freshen up a bit. *Why?* I have no idea because it's not like he hasn't seen me at my worst.

Coming into the kitchen, wrapped in my robe, I see he has already made coffee. "If I didn't know any better, I'd think this was your place," I say, taking my coffee. "I was supposed to be making this for us."

"You can still put your cream on my bagel." He winks, almost making me drop my mug.

"I mean, the bagel still needs cream cheese," he rephrases his sentence, noticing the change in my body language.

"Have you tried a cream cheese and strawberry jam combination? It's delicious,"

I say, going into the kitchen. "Let me make it for you."

"I'm down to try anything once."

"I remember," I say, walking back into the living room.

"So," I pause as I sit back down, "would you like to…."

"Like to…what?" Desmond says after waiting longer than he should have for me to ask my question.

"Go have that dinner soon. You know, to have *that* talk?"

"I would love to." He beams. "Just tell me when, and I'll be there."

"Great!" I blush.

"I should probably get going," Desmond says, taking the last bite of his bagel. "I think I've overstayed my welcome."

"You didn't." The words come rushing from my lips faster than my brain can process.

"I'm happy to know you still like having me around."

"I almost forgot how much I enjoyed being in your presence."

"Well, maybe we can fix that, but only if your boyfriend is okay with it. Congrats on the baby, by the way. Motherhood is going to suit you well."

Fuck, I do have a whole boyfriend who I just completely forgot about that fast. I'm a horrible person—the worst.

"Um, he isn't the jealous type. I'm sure he'd be fine with it," I lie, ignoring his comments about the baby and me.

Looking at my first love, I couldn't help but feel like I was making the wrong decision. I had decided to go through with the pregnancy, but seeing him standing in front of me made me wonder if I had made the right choice. It was supposed to be him—no one else.

"Good to know. I should get going. I need to shower and get ready for a training session. Can I call you later?" He asks, walking towards the door.

"I'll text you first," I say, reaching for his hand before he walks out the door. "Thank you." I acknowledge his words from earlier before hugging him goodbye.

16

See You Later

Saturday, March 18, 2006

Desmond

"I guess it's time for me to say goodbye now," Skye whines.

She's been at my place every night since we've met, and I wouldn't have it any other way. She prepares the perfect bowl of ramen, bakes the softest chocolate chip cookies, and tidies up after herself. She even helps me fold my laundry after I wash it—something about getting anxiety from looking at a pile of perfectly clean clothes. When I roll over and see her in my bed, my next thought isn't, *is this chick ever going to leave?* Having her in my space brings me peace.

From the moment I saw Skye, we became inseparable. At 5'2", she was petite but carried herself like a six-foot goddess. She was royalty. Her gentle brown eyes drew me in from across the room, and I longed for her to come closer. I was intrigued by how she moved—every fiber of my being yearned for her.

"I don't like the word goodbye."

"And why is that?" Skye stands on her tippy toes and wraps her arms around my neck.

"Because goodbyes seem final, and I never want what we have to end," I say, kissing her forehead.

"Aww. I think you might love me." She uses my shoulders to lift herself and wraps her legs around me, hugging me tight.

Her words ring true to my ears. I fell the moment I saw her, but I'll wait a little longer to say those three words. I'm not trying to run her off, but I'm confident she feels the same.

"Don't get ahead of yourself."

"Anyways," she pauses, "what am I supposed to say if I can't say goodbye to you?"

"I'll see you later."

"Okay then. I'll see you later, Desmond Walker."

"Tonight at 7:00 PM, be here at my door dressed in a sexy black dress," I demand.

"Are you finally taking me on a date?" She blushes.

"Yes. I'm taking you on a date, Skye."

"I'm looking forward to it," she says, gazing into my eyes. "As much as I love cuddling up to you all day and night, I need you to know that I'm more than just a sweatpants and crop top kind of girl." She giggles and then kisses me on the lips.

I savor the moment, holding her tightly as she tries to wiggle her way from my grip. I'd spend all day with her wrapped around me like this if I could.

"How can I return if you refuse to let me go? At this rate, I'll never be able to get back to my room to change."

"You're the one who jumped your little ass up here and about that...I'm counting on you moving in."

"You'd have to ask me first," she says, gazing into my eyes. "Plus, you've only known me for two months. You might get tired of me."

"You've been here every night since we've met, and I'm not tired of you yet. So, do you want to move in?" I ask.

"I'd need to be your girlfriend first." She pats my chest and escapes from my arms. Dashing out the door without letting me say another word.

"I'm going to do just that," I say to myself, closing the door behind her. The time had come to make her my lady, officially. Most would say I'm rushing into things, but my mind is made up, and nothing can change that.

<u>17</u>

Emotionally His

Sunday, November 14, 2010

Skye

Closing the door behind me, I brace myself against it, feeling my knees give way as I sink to the floor. I can't stop the tears from streaming down my face as I hold myself tightly. So many emotions are swirling inside me, and I feel lost. Our night together was supposed to bring closure, not leave me feeling alone and confused.

My heart is in turmoil just thinking about him. It's hard to resist the pull of emotions, but I can't keep ignoring the elephant following me around. We lost something precious and never truly acknowledged it. There was so much left unsaid between us, which was why I invited him over to confront it. I didn't intend to fall back into our old routines and forget to address us.

I'm with Lance physically, but it's so obvious my heart belongs to someone else. I can try to deny it over and over again, but Desmond is the one who has my heart. It's a fucked-up situation. Lance doesn't deserve to be in this position. One he doesn't even know he's in. He doesn't deserve for me to be running after a man I claimed to be over.

Picking myself up off the floor, I rush over to my phone. I'd been snuggled up on the couch in this apartment with Desmond and hadn't checked my cell once. When I sent the text inviting Desmond over, I put my phone on silent and left it on my nightstand for the rest of the night. I never thought about going to check it, which was stupid. *What would I have done if Lance got off work early and showed up at my door?* It's not like he has a key, but it would be suspicious as fuck to turn him away or not answer at all. I always answer.

Of course, there was a text from Emily telling me how everything with Jordan was worked out and that she'd be making an appointment to get her breasts examined.

Lance hadn't reached out to me like I thought he would. He called once and sent me a text telling me he would come by in the afternoon after waking up from his nap. There was a voice in me saying, "Tell him no," but I would have to devise an excuse for not wanting to see him.

"BINGO," I yell out, remembering it's Sunday. He should be spending today with his mom instead of coming to see me. He'll invite me along, but I could tell him I'm tired, a little sick, and just wanted to spend the day resting.

"Yeah, that should work," I say to myself.

Skye: Good morning, babe. After you rest, you should visit your mom today. I've been nauseous and exhausted. Are you okay with me taking some time to myself today?

Straight to the point!

After placing my phone down, I make my way to the shower. Desmond's aroma still lingers in the air—a unique blend of masculinity and sweetness that never fails

to make me feel euphoric. As I inhale
deeply, my body reacts with a delightful
tingling sensation that sends shivers down
my spine.

"God, he smells good."

~

Lance: *Sure!*

Once I got dressed and finished cleaning
up, I eventually received a text from Lance.
As soon as I saw the word, *sure*, with
nothing to follow, I sensed something was
off. What the hell does *sure* mean?

I hadn't planned on telling Emily about
Desmond coming over, let alone tell her he
had spent the night, but I needed someone
to vent to. I headed straight to her
restaurant when I got dressed. She'd be
closing up when I arrived and could give
me her undivided attention.

"Do you think he knows?"

"Knows that I had my ex-boyfriend over,
practically drooling over him…literally and
figuratively? That's impossible," I say,

spitting my words out at the speed of light. "Don't you think he would have said something? Came kicking down the door?"

"Can you relax and have a seat, please." Emily stands up and grabs me by the arms once I walk back toward her. "All that movement is making me nervous."

"You're nervous?" I yell, placing my hands on my hips, "I'm the nervous one… I'm probably fucked. You sure I can't have one little drink?"

"No, Skye! You cannot have one little drink. You're pregnant, remember?"

"How can I forget?" I say, taking a deep breath. "Desmond reminded me of that right before he walked out my door."

"He's trying to keep things friendly. It would be weird for him not to acknowledge the pregnancy."

"How can he so easily acknowledge this pregnancy when he couldn't even acknowledge the pregnancy we lost?"

Another detail I swore I would never share was again out in the open.

Emily pauses. I can see she is struggling internally. I can't determine if she's upset with me for keeping such a secret from her or if she feels bad for me. As I'm about to speak, she pulls me into her and holds me tight.

"How come I didn't know?" Her voice scratches. "I should have noticed. Am I that shitty of a friend?"

I can feel the dampness on my shirt from her tears falling onto my chest, and the feeling is all too familiar. The tears pouring from her face are the emotions I felt when I lost everything precious to me—heartbroken, devastated, and guilty. But Emily has nothing to feel guilty about. The one who should feel guilty is me. I kept the miscarriage from her, not fully trusting that she could be there for me.

Emily, with all good intentions, always had a way of making everything about her. She doesn't do it purposefully, but it's one of the reasons I keep certain aspects of my life to myself. Don't get it wrong, Emily has always been a great friend to me despite that minor flaw, and I hope she knows that. Her love for me has always been evident, but she just doesn't know how to remove herself from certain equations. But again, that's my fault. I know Emily is sensitive, so I never call her out when I notice her making herself the center of attention. I just started to withhold information precious to me—my unborn was just that. I couldn't bring myself to tell her—to share my pain. I didn't want it to become hers and then there be the possibility of me having to hold in my emotions to put hers back together.

"No one knew, Em."

"But I should have," she expresses, squeezing me tighter.

"Desmond and I planned on telling everyone about my pregnancy, eventually. I promise. We had a surprise party ready to go, but I lost the baby before that could happen. After that, I wanted to focus on getting through the pain."

"I could have been there for you, Skye." Emily pulls away from me, wiping the tears from her eyes. "I could have helped you through it all."

"You wouldn't have been able to do anything for me, Emily. Desmond couldn't," I admit.

"Is this why you broke up with him?" Emily takes my hand.

"I guess so." I pause for a minute, remembering when everything about us changed. "He wasn't the man I needed him to be during my time of need."

"He could have been grieving too, and I'm not trying to be rude, but you probably pushed him away without knowing," Emily says.

I don't know why, but those words rub me the wrong way despite how true they may be. I guess I'm not the only sensitive one in this friend group. Either way, my pushing him away isn't something I want to discuss today, not when there's a possibility of my current relationship crumbling like the last.

"Maybe," I say quickly. "Is there someone here that can make us something to eat?"

"I'll take that as my cue to stop talking and make you something," Emily says, walking toward the back and entering the kitchen of her restaurant.

"Thank you."

<u>18</u>

Out of Time

Saturday, December 18, 2010

Skye

Christmas was a week away, and I hadn't put up one ornament or bought anyone a gift. Typically, I would have decorations and lights covering every inch of my apartment when the Thanksgiving table was cleared, but the spirit hasn't quite hit me this year.

I barely celebrated Thanksgiving. Lance had work, and I wasn't going to drive back home to my parents. Instead, I went to have an early dinner with him and his mom before he had to get ready to head into the city. Then I came home, curled up under my covers, and watched a ton of movies until I physically couldn't keep my eyes open any longer.

If Emily saw how bare my apartment was, she'd try to check me into the hospital. Luckily, she's been busy planning her engagement party. After she and Jordan had that little misunderstanding, he proposed to her the next day. Emily loves saying my living room looks like it vomited an entire Christmas village. I take it as a compliment. My mother wasn't big on decorations, and my dad always worked. She would throw up a tree and some stockings, then call it decorating. I told myself I would live in a truly magical home that looked like the houses in a Hallmark movie.

It'll be my first Christmas with Lance, but I'm not as excited as I thought. Nowhere near as excited as I was when Desmond and I spent our first Christmas together. It was so cute. I went all out for him. This year I'd rather spend time in my reindeer pajamas watching romantic holiday movies and eating cookies and caramel popcorn from a tin, but my mother insisted I show up at my aunt's house on Christmas day. She was even nice enough to invite Lance along, even though she despises him for being the person I decided to be with.

I hadn't introduced him to the rest of the family, and she said Christmas would be the perfect day. Apparently, Christmas puts everyone in a good mood, but my family is full of Grinches in disguise. What I pictured in my head was a shit show.

I was already slightly picking up weight in my hips and breasts. I could play it off by saying I've been eating out more than usual, but eventually, I'll have to tell her she'll be a grandmother. I'm terrified of her reaction. My father will look around stupidly because, just like me, he seems to be scared of her, or maybe he's just learned how to tune her out after all these years. I don't understand how a man that sweet ended up with a witch like her.

The only person she's ever been nice to is Desmond, which was always weird. I expected her to give him the hardest time. I had started to think she had a crush on him. Desmond always said I was being dramatic, but if he liked older women and she wasn't

married to my dad, she'd take a stab at him.
Sometimes, I wished they would have
divorced as a kid so I could go live with
him, but knowing my mom, she would
have made my dad's life a living hell until
he died.

> ***Emily:*** *Have you decided on what you're*
> *wearing to our Christmas Eve/Engagement*
> *party?*

> ***Skye:*** *No. I'll find something out of the*
> *closet.*

> ***Emily:*** *And risk Desmond seeing you in a*
> *repeater. I don't think so. Be ready in an*
> *hour. We're going shopping, and there will*
> *be no crying this time.*

"Fuck," I say out loud, putting down my
phone.

I forgot Desmond was going to be at the
Christmas Eve party. I told Lance he
wouldn't be there, and now I'll look like a
liar. Why did I even say that stupid shit? Of
course, Desmond was going to be at the
party. Jordan is his best friend.

Duh, Skye! I think and knock myself upside the head. *Pregnancy brain can't be kicking in this soon. I wonder if he's going to bring a plus one.*

Watching him with another woman would be my hell. It serves me right for leaving him the way I did…At least that's what my mama would say. Hopefully, Emily gave him the same treatment Jordan was giving me. I asked Emily if Lance could come, but the answer was no. Jordan made it clear that he would never allow me to bring another man around him.

I thought it was ridiculous, but "Bro Code."

~

Lance

I'm starting to think our relationship isn't going to work. I saw her ex walking out of her apartment a month ago, and I knew my time was running out. I could have popped up on her anytime, but she obviously didn't care about getting caught in her place, *alone*, with her ex-boyfriend. The shit is disrespectful. I wanted to run up on that nigga and lay him on his ass for having the balls to even try to get close to her again, but I refused to fight like a dog in the streets over a woman confused about what and who she wants to be with.

I wondered if he had been there all night, sleeping next to my woman, holding her close like she was still his—if this had transpired more than once. I knew the nigga lived up the street, but I trusted her enough to know she would never allow him to come through. Their living close was the first detail she spilled about him. She wanted me to be aware of who he was in case we ever had a run-in with one another. Currently, I can't help but imagine that nigga being over there every time I was at work. Those graveyard shifts would have allowed him plenty of time to pull up on my woman and put dick in her.

I thought me and Skye had a strong foundation, but the minute I saw that *she loves me still,* smile across that nigga's face, all my confidence went out the window. Just like that, my spot was gone. He was about to be the beginning of our end. He was her true love. I, on the other hand, was supposed to be a quick fuck. I'm starting to wish we left it at that, but now she's carrying my seed—a boy, I hope.

Is the baby mine?

That thought leaves me once I realize Skye isn't that kind of girl. There's no way she would be fucking on another man and then laying up with me. That would be some fucked up shit, and that'll be the day someone has to bail me out of jail.

Sorry mama.

I shouldn't even be with a woman I'm doubting. I know she's noticed I've been distant lately, but I use exhaustion as an excuse, and she doesn't seem to mind. I wouldn't either if I had a rekindled love interest. Lately, I've taken on more shifts, not because I need money but to steer clear of her and avoid any discussions about him. My emotions are running high right now, and I'm unwilling to unjustly lash out at her. I've been taking the time to consider how I want this relationship to play out.

We're supposed to be spending Christmas Day together, her favorite holiday. It'll be our first Christmas as a couple, and I'm supposed to meet the rest of her family, but I'm not sure that's a good idea. Her mama doesn't even like me, and I'm sure she's told the family I'm just some guy her daughter is using to get over her ex.

When I met her mother, she kept her love for Desmond no secret. She couldn't stop mentioning the man's name. Anyone in their right mind should have seen that as a sign of the deep connection between him, Skye, and her family, but I sat there through all the disrespect. It wasn't on me to put that woman in her place. My mom taught me how to respect my elders.

I'm sure Mrs. Rose still doesn't know about Skye being pregnant, seeing as they don't exactly talk on the regular. On top of that, she cursed me out for telling my mom about it, and they're close to one another.

Maybe she doesn't want this baby, I think as I pull out my phone.

<u>19</u>

What About Us

Saturday, December 18, 2010

Skye

While shopping with Emily, I received a text from Lance saying we needed to talk. It's either good news or something terrible when someone tells you they need to speak to you. In my heart, I knew the conversation was only leading to one outcome—Lance and I breaking up.

I was right!

"You don't want me to have the baby?" I'm sitting on the bed in a puddle of tears, looking up at Lance.

I'm caught off guard.

He went from wanting to scream from the mountain tops about becoming a dad— reading through parenting books and picking out baby names to telling me he no longer wants me to have his child. I saw the breakup coming, but I wasn't prepared for this.

Initially, I was skeptical, but once I came around to the idea of being a mom, I was thrilled to have a second chance at motherhood. Now he wants to take it from me.

"I thought about it, and we should cut all ties. I'm not raising a child in two separate homes, and I don't want anyone coming around trying to play daddy in the future. An abortion will be better for both of us."

Standing up, I use all my might to push him as far away from me as possible. How dare he decide this for me? He's only doing what's best for him. I don't want to look at him. I don't want to speak to him. I don't want him here anymore. Because I trusted him, I chose to continue the journey. He made me feel like he'd be there for me no matter what—including a potential separation in the future. It's not like he was planning on marrying me any time soon. We haven't even been together for a year. Us being together forever was never a guarantee.

The last thing I anticipated was the scene in front of me—him standing in my face, telling me I should get an abortion.

"I'll pay for it if you're worried about the money."

"Wow. Are you fucking kidding me? You're serious, aren't you? If you didn't want me to have the baby, why in the fuck would you tell your mom? Why make me believe you wanted a family with me?"

"I was excited. Happy for us to be creating a life together," he pauses, "until I saw that nigga coming out of your apartment like he lived in that muthafucka. Taking out the trash with a big ass smile on his face."

And there it was, the reason Lance had been keeping our conversations short. He didn't want to stay the night in my bed anymore and was side-eyeing me when he thought I wasn't looking. Lance was upset about Desmond, and he had a right to be. I had another man, and not just any man, a man I was madly in love with, a man I'm still in love with, in the space that was supposed to be me and his.

"I can explain." I stand up and walk toward him, but he backs away.

"I opened myself up to you. I welcomed you into my mother's home. I made space for you in my heart," he says, looking me up and down, "and you still had unresolved feelings for the next man the whole time."

"Lance, I was with him for four years. Feelings don't evaporate that fast."

"If that's the case, how long have you been seeing him behind my back?"

"I haven't been seeing him."

"You're lying, Skye. I came to your place after work and saw him leaving with my own eyes."

"That was his first and only time being here," I say, reaching for his hands, but he pushes mine away.

I've never seen Lance this upset. We barely have disagreements, and now he doubts everything I've ever felt for him. I know I'm wrong for inviting Desmond over here, but I had to see…I needed to see if what I thought I was feeling was still there—and it was, but I was willing to extinguish the flames for the life growing inside me…a life with Lance.

"Well, this will be the last time you see me." He turns toward the door.

"What about the baby? What about us?" I yell and run toward him, grabbing his arm right before he reaches the front door.

"Skye," he says, tears filling his eyes, "there is no us. There was never supposed to be an *us*."

"And the baby?"

"The choice is yours, but I prefer we not create a broken family," he says, walking out the door.

<u>20</u>

Christmas Eve

Friday, December 24, 2010

Skye

Tonight is the engagement party. Do I want to go? Not exactly, but I'd be the worst friend ever if I missed out on Emily's beautiful night. I just know she went all out. Even if Lance and I hadn't broken up, it's not like he would have been there by my side.

Celebrating love when I no longer have it is a bittersweet feeling.

Unfortunately for me, staying home isn't an option. Emily will dump me like Lance did if I don't show up. I haven't had the chance to tell her how he left me and, on top of that, asked me to get an abortion. Subconsciously, I wanted our relationship to end, but I was hoping it would be on my terms if it indeed came to that. Tomorrow will be a week, and I haven't heard from him once. I didn't think it would be that easy for him to walk away.

Walking into the kitchen, I grab a wine glass from the cabinet and open the fridge to grab a bottle of wine. Once my hand is wrapped around the bottle, I start to cry — cry because the reality that I'm about to become a single mom kicks in.

I shouldn't be a mom at all, I think as I pull the bottle out of the fridge and sit it on the counter. I stare at it for a while before opening it.

"You can't drink that, Skye," I hear a voice say, my voice. "I guess I haven't completely lost it," I say, pouring the wine down the sink. The smell attacks me, and suddenly, I have the urge to throw up everything I didn't eat.

Rushing toward the bathroom, I push the door open and drop to my knees in front of the toilet bowl. The floor is cold and uncomfortable, but I don't have time to ponder on that. My body convulses as fluid pours from my throat. It hurts because there's nothing left in me to expel, but the feeling doesn't go away. My body continues to extract whatever it can from within me. Leaning against the bathtub, I wipe my mouth, and then I cry—cry because I feel drained of all of my energy and because all of this is my fault.

Why couldn't I be on my own? Why did I rush into a relationship I knew I wasn't ready for? Why didn't I work on myself so that I could make my way back to Desmond?

Getting off the floor, I flush the toilet, wash my hands, and brush my teeth. Walking back toward the tub, I begin to run a bath. Pouring my favorite eucalyptus bubbles in. I'm not supposed to bathe in hot water while pregnant but fuck it. I probably won't be keeping this baby anyway. I want to do things correctly. I want to be in love with myself, the seed growing inside me, and the man who helped plant it. Emily was getting at something the day she asked if I was in love. I wasn't. I just loved the idea of recreating what I had with Desmond. Having a baby with Lance wouldn't make up for the one I lost.

"Damn it," I yell when I hear the water spilling over.

~

Pulling into the mansion's driveway, it looked like I was entering a winter wonderland. It was magical. At any second, Angels would appear, and snow would begin to fall. My heart felt warm, and these were the vibes I needed. I cried for hours while trying to get myself together for this event, but I managed to get here, and thank goodness, because the photo ops will be heavenly.

Opening the door, the valet grabs my hand and helps me exit the vehicle. He hands me a tag with a number, and I put it in my purse. Making my way up the steps, I'm greeted by a massive picture of Emily and Jordan, wearing all white. They look so young and in love. They look like innocent children who believe that nothing else in the world matters except for the love they share. I remembered how I used to look at

Desmond with those same eyes. So full of love, life, beauty, and hope.

"Are you going to go in or just look at that picture all night?" His deep, sensual voice sent a chill through me, making me blush.

Who knew the sound escaping his lips would change my mood drastically?

Laughing, I say, "Can I not admire the beauty before me?"

"Admire that beautiful face as much as you want, but it looks better up close and personal," Emily's voice echoes.

She is standing at the entry doors at the top of the steps in a long, strapless dress that sparkles at every twist and turn. She looks like she walked out of a Disney movie. She's the beauty, and Jordan is the beast. I can't take my eyes off her. There is no doubt that Emily could be a runway model, but tonight, she's beyond a dream.

"Pick up your lip," Desmond says, grabbing my hand. Happily, I welcome his embrace as he walks me inside. Jordan winks at Desmond, and Emily grins. The four of us walk into the party together, just like old times.

~

Desmond

"Exquisite," I say, watching Skye trek up the stairs.

She has her hair in a neat bun on the top of her head, secured with designer bobby pins. They look like diamonds in her hair as they twinkle under the Christmas lights. The black sequin dress she has on hugs her petite frame like a glove. She may be covered entirely, but the way the dress clings to her, I can't help but let my mind wander to places I haven't been since she left.

I haven't been involved with any other woman since Skye officially called it quits, nor have I wanted to. The chemistry she and I had will never be matched. I don't think I could find anyone that would come close to my beautiful Skye. I hold onto the idea of us getting a second chance, but for now, I have to respect that she's with someone else.

I watch as she studies the picture of Emily and Jordan. They took it on their fifth anniversary. The day they had me take the photos, Jordan said one day it would be used for their engagement. Watching him be that in love that young made me sick, but now I understand that need. I know what it feels like to want to die if that person ever left your side. I've been slowly dying every day I've spent without Skye. She revived me when she asked me to come over to her place. I planned to get the closure that night, but instead, it seemed like our ending could be our new beginning.

"Are you going to go in or just look at that picture all night?" I step close and whisper in her ear. For a second, she appears frozen, as if time is standing still, but then those chubby cheekbones lift, and I get a glimpse of her deep dimple.

Laughing, she turns and says, "Can I not admire the beauty before me?"

My mind is telling me to caress her face and tell her she is the most beautiful woman I've ever seen, but the sound of Emily's voice stops me. It's probably a good thing. After briefly speaking, it's time for us to go inside to celebrate our best friends. I put out my arm, and Skye instinctively interlocked her arm with mine, just as she had the year before. It was like deja vu, and I enjoyed every minute.

<u>21</u>

Christmas Day

Saturday, December 25, 2010
Skye

Last night was perfect. I danced, laughed, shed tears of joy, and caught up with old friends. There was no talk of babies, and I didn't have to spill the tea about Lance breaking up with me. The night was filled with love and happiness. I appreciated how much Jordan cherished the ground Emily walked on.

Desmond and I were practically joined at the hip all night, confusing those who passed by. We laughed hysterically when we were mistaken for a couple here and there. The looks on their faces when we said, "We're only friends," was all the entertainment I needed. Our connection was there, and part of me wanted to spend the entire night with him, but I couldn't go there. I did my best to stay till the end but was exhausted. Desmond walked me out front to get my car from valet, and once I was gone, he texted me to make sure I arrived home safely.

Mom: I hope you're up so you can be on your way to your aunts.

Skye: It's 8 in the morning.

Mom: I know what time it is. Now get your hungover ass up so you can start helping us cook.

I wish I were hungover. I'd have an excuse not to deal with your ass.

I don't bother texting her back. If only she knew I hadn't been drinking because the fetus resting in my womb. At times, I wonder why God paired me with that woman. For her to be the woman who carried me for nine months and spent two days in labor with me, I sure don't feel any connection to her.

Two hours later, I'm pulling up to my aunt's house. My first thought is to turn around and drive back home. Anything would be better than being here. I put my car in reverse, and before I can back out, I'm blocked in by a bright red Honda Civic.

There goes my chance of escaping.

Opening my car door, I'm greeted by my cousin. She may be the only sane woman on my mother's side of the family. I don't see her much, but she makes these visits worth it.

"I can't believe you were about to leave me with these bitter-ass women on Christmas Day," she says, hugging me.

"I would never," I lie.

"Bitch please, I know a getaway in progress when I see one." She laughs. "Want to smoke before we go in?"

"Now you know damn well my mom would have a fit, and I don't want to hear her shit," I say.

"I see she's still trying to ruin your life."

"Every chance she gets." I shake my head.

Entering the house, I brace myself for impact. The first comment that comes out of her mouth will be about Lance. I already have my lie prepared. I won't be telling them I'm a single woman. Not today.

"Merry Christmas," I chirp as I enter the family room.

The men are on the couch watching football, and as I predicted, my mom and aunt are in the kitchen cooking and gossiping per usual. I approach my uncles first. I know they'll shower me with love, and it's just what I need. They know to mind their business.

"Merry Christmas, baby girl. It's so good to see you."

"You too, Uncle Lou. You're looking mighty young these days." I kiss him.

"...and what about me," my Uncle Al chimes in.

"Unc, you know damn well you're a lady killer."

"Stop boosting those old men's egos and come in here and help us," I hear my mom yell from across the room.

Unknowingly, my eyes roll behind my head, and my uncles laugh.

"You bet not be over there rolling them big ass eyes," she yells.

"Got damn, Lina, the girl just got here. Give her a chance to relax. You know she just spent two hours in that damn car," Uncle Lou yells.

That's my mom's brother, and he always has my back. My mom can't stand it, but he doesn't give a damn. He never had a child, so I've always been like a daughter to him.

"Oh shut up, Lou," she yells.

"Thank you," I mouth to my uncle before walking into the kitchen.

My aunt is cleaning the crab for the gumbo, and my mom is making her famous mac-n-cheese.

"Nice to see you too, Mom," I say, hugging her awkwardly. Affection has never been our thing. Well, it was never her thing, but I learned to get used to it.

"Where's that little boyfriend of yours?" She asks like I knew she would. "I thought you would introduce him to the family today."

"He decided to spend the day with his mom," I tell a slight lie because I don't want to reveal the truth about our breakup. "It's her first Christmas without her husband, and he wanted to be there for her."

"Where did her husband go?"

"He died. I'm pretty sure I told you this already."

"Must not have listened."

"Do you ever?" I mumble and make my way toward my aunt. I'd do anything to avoid an argument with my mom. "Need help with anything?"

"Thanks for asking," she says, then cuts her eyes at my cousin. "Do you mind starting the roux for me?"

"You would give me the time-consuming task," I say before taking off my coat.

"Do you even know what you're doing?" My mom says with judgment in her voice, so much for avoiding confrontation. She can't help but criticize and question my every move.

"Yes, I know what I'm doing. She wouldn't have asked me if I didn't."

"I guess, but I ain't never seen you cook nothing a day in your life," she says in a tone that ticks me off.

"Why did you ask me here if you're going to be such a bitch?"

The words leave my mouth before my brain takes the time to register what to say. My mother and I indeed have a rocky relationship, but I've never fixed my lips to call her out of her name. At least not out loud. I feel all eyes on me, but it's too late to take it back—neither do I want to.

"Skye!" My aunt gasps.

"Fellas, I think that's our cue to go outside and enjoy a cigar," my Uncle Lou says.

"I'm sorry, Auntie, but she always has something negative to say. I just walked in here. I've barely been here for 5 minutes, and instead of acting like she's happy to see me, she spews all these smart-ass remarks at me, and for what?"

"Skye, baby, she's your mom, and even though she can be unkind at times, you still need to respect her," my aunt tries to reason.

"I'm a grown-ass woman, and I don't have to put up with her shit. I shouldn't have to respect her if she can't respect me." I pause for a second and look at my mom. "If you were going to hate me so much, you should have aborted me. It would have been better than dealing with a mom who acts like she wants no parts of me."

"Maybe you're right. You're a disappointment," she points her finger at me, "and you lost the only good thing going for you."

She stopped what she was doing and walked closer to me. She's so close I can smell the eggnog and vodka on her breath. The rage coming from her glossy brown eyes is hot enough to burn the house down. I'm afraid of what she will say—do, but I can't back down now.

"You still live in a little ole apartment, working freelance jobs, pretending like you're happy. When are you going to get a real job, a career? Not that damn writing and website-building shit you do. Do you have no real goals in life?"

"Wow, fuck you," I yell, throwing the apron toward her, happy my dad isn't here to see this shit show. "I have a career. Maybe it's not the one you picked for me, but it's one that makes me happy. One that gives me the luxury of working the hours I want, traveling where I want, and most of all, it got me from under your fucking control."

"No, fuck you, little girl. I can't wait to tell your dad what a little bitch you were today. I told him spoiling you would be a mistake."

"Lina," my aunt gasps in disbelief. "You need to relax. We're supposed to enjoy each other's company, not go for each other's throats."

"Nah, it's cool auntie. Let her true feelings fly."

"Want me to move my car?" My cousin asks. She's the one person who knows I'm not willing to sit around awkwardly to please anyone, especially my mother.

"Please." I snatch my jacket out of the chair. "Next time you invite me somewhere, make sure that woman is buried six feet deep first."

"You've done it this time, Lina," I hear my aunt say before I close the door behind me and run to my car.

I've argued with my mom, but never like this.

Not wanting to ruin anyone's holiday, I pull out my phone and text the only person I know will come to my aid, no questions asked.

> **Skye:** *Are you free in about 3 hours? Can you come to my place?*

~

Desmond

Christmas is cool, but it's never been my thing. I don't wake up excited or anything close to it. When my parents passed away, I didn't see the point in celebrating anymore. I had lost the only family worth celebrating holidays like this with. So, once the holidays came around, I would spend Christmas Eve with my college friends if they were in town—like last night, and on Christmas, I would wake up, make breakfast, and take the day to myself.

Sometimes, I'd take a long drive, going from town to town to look at the lights. Other times, I'd kick back, listen to music, and roll up.

That was until I met Skye.

She nearly took my head off when I told her I don't celebrate Christmas. From that day forward, she included me in all her family events, and they always welcomed me with open arms. I miss that family dynamic, even if it sometimes gets slightly dysfunctional. I'm sure she's with them, getting ready to enjoy a big bowl of gumbo while I lay here starving.

The first year I spent Christmas with them was my and Skye's second Christmas together. Her mom refused to let me miss it again. It took her almost two years just to introduce me to her family. I'm guessing she wanted to make sure we were really in the relationship for the long haul. Well, that Christmas, her mom and auntie had me in the kitchen chopping up food as they dug deep for anything they could use against me—something to prove I wasn't good enough for their Skye. Her mom hoped I was some young fool she could talk her daughter out of being with, but she fell for me immediately.

Skye couldn't stand it. She hated how easy it was for her mom to be kind and loving toward me when she couldn't always provide that same comfort to Skye. I always figured it came from me not having my parents.

I thought about texting Skye to say Merry Christmas, but I figured she'd be with her man. I wanted to reach out to her mom too, but I don't need her getting pissed at me.

I wonder if her family likes him.

Skye mentioned she hadn't had the best relationship with her mother before letting me meet her, but whenever I came around, she seemed to have a massive smile—happy to be around her daughter. They would laugh and reminisce on old times. Like the time Skye entered a talent show and won first place. They even had the video and a VHS setup prepared to show me. She was so tiny and adorable.

My phone goes off, and the chime pierces my ear, causing my head to start pounding.

After walking Skye to her car, I stayed at the party a bit longer, taking shots with old friends. I'm suffering for it today, but at least I can chill—no kids to watch open gifts, no parents to listen to bickering, and no girlfriend to spoil. All I have is me, a nice shower, some pain relievers, and my bed.

Reaching over, I take my phone to check the message that came through. To my surprise, it was the one person I'd been thinking of all night.

> **Skye:** *Are you free in about 3 hours? Can you come to my place?*

> **Desmond:** *Merry Christmas! Of course. See you soon.*

"Damn, nigga! Can you not sound so desperate?" I say as I quickly get out of bed, shower, and get dressed.

I pull the sweater that Skye got for me out of the closet. We were supposed to do the whole ugly sweater thing this year, but back then, she didn't realize she'd be over us within a month. A few days after Christmas, she dragged me out of bed and to every store still selling Christmas items, telling me this was the perfect time to get everything we needed for next year because everything would be on clearance.

Not even on my drunkest night did I think I'd be wearing this ugly ass sweater or getting to bring in another Christmas with her, but I'm grateful. She always had a way of making the holidays magical.

The first Christmas we spent together—I was convinced she was crazy. As soon as Thanksgiving ended, she went straight into Christmas mode. She forced me to buy an artificial tree covered in white glittery snow. She decorated every corner of my apartment from ceiling to floor. It was a lot, but her joy was worth the glitter and lights.

That year, we went ice skating, knowing I'd never been skating a day in my life. I was terrified, and though Skye found my struggle amusing, by the end of the night, she was jealous of how good I had gotten.

"It took me years to ice skate like that," she whined.

That same year, we did a Christmas lights tour, and she even talked me into taking pictures with Santa—a grown-ass man taking pictures with Santa Claus.

It's a Christmas I'll always cherish.

22

Ex-Factors

Skye

Kicking off my shoes and throwing my purse to the floor, I run to the bathroom to relieve myself. I can't hold water or any other liquid these days. I should have peed before storming out of my aunt's house, but I couldn't look at my mother for another second. She was wrong, and I stand on that.

Usually, we would keep the drama between the two of us, but now the whole family will be talking about it, and I won't even be there to defend myself. I know my Uncle Lou is going to put her in her place. He don't play that shit. He said mom has had that same attitude since she was a kid—picking fights with the girls at school, giving my grandma a hard time just for the hell of it. Granny even kicked her out once until she came begging to return home. They said it was the perfect attitude adjustment until she could finally leave for good. Lina knew who and who not to get smart with. Granny didn't tolerate disrespect. Like my mom, she expected the best from her kids—good grades, an extensive education, manners, and a whole lot of drive. At least one of them got it right.

Maybe after our argument, she'll be nicer to me. I've never approached her the way I had today. I always try my best to be respectful since she is my mother.

Changing into something more comfortable, I tidy up the mess I left behind when I rushed out of the house. I still can't get over how I wasted my time and gas traveling miles to end up back in my apartment. My ugly-ass undecorated apartment.

After lighting a few candles, I grab my throw blanket and turn on Hallmark. Nothing catches my eye, so I turn on a classic, **Home Alone**. As Kevin yells at his entire family and prays for them to disappear, I yell at the TV, "I get it, kid, I get it."

The doorbell rings in the middle of my rant, and I immediately feel flutters. Pulling down my sweater and adjusting my hair, I walk toward the door, but for some reason, I become frozen. My hand is on the knob but refusing to move. It rings again, this time making me jump.

Get it together. It's only Desmond.

When I open the door, our eyes fall directly on our sweaters. Looking up at him, I smile, and he laughs.

"Are you going to invite me in, twin?"

Shaking myself back to reality, I speak. "How rude of me? Sorry, come on in."

I didn't notice the two bags in Desmond's hands because I was stuck on the ugly gingerbread man on his sweater, asking me if I wanted a taste. I bought the same. I thought he would have thrown it out after our breakup.

"What's in the bag?" I ask.

Walking into the kitchen, he begins unpacking the items from the bag. "I brought marshmallows, hot chocolate, chocolate chip cookie dough, milk, and a few things to make us some dinner," he says.

"You didn't have to bring all of this?"

"But I felt like I had to, and from the looks of this apartment, I think I was right," he says, looking around. "Where are the hanging lights, stockings, elves, and your mini-Christmas tree? And why aren't you with your family?"

I ignore his questions and ask, "What's in that box?"

"This one?" He says, picking up the shoe-like box covered in glitter and handing it to me. "Open it and see."

Did he get me a Christmas gift?

I take hold of the box and walk over to the sofa. Slowly opening it, my heart starts to beat a little differently, like it did the day I laid eyes on him. I don't want to feel this way. I should be sad right now. I should be angry at the man who left me the week before and told me to forget about him and our baby. I should be in another city, sharing stories and eating gumbo with my family. I should be doing and feeling many things, and none of those are supposed to involve Desmond.

I broke it off with him, so why am I even sitting here…on top of the world?

"Did I do good?" Desmond asks, pulling me out of my thoughts.

"Perfect!" I turn to him and smile.

Inside the box is an envelope that reads, "Don't open me until I leave," two scented candles that would make the Grinch a fan of Christmas, a mini plush Mrs. Clause, and my favorite movie, *A Diva's Christmas Carol.*

"We are watching this immediately," I say, holding the movie in the air.

"How about you finish watching Home Alone? I'll cook, and then we can watch it."

"I hope it's something delicious because I am starving," I say, rubbing my stomach.

~

Desmond

Moving around her kitchen, I see everything has stayed the same. It's like being in my apartment when she lived there. She couldn't help but rearrange everything to suit her needs.

The pots and pans are still in the bottom cabinets near the oven. She has built-in wall shelves that keep all the spices she moved from the original jars into glass jars with specialized labels. Her cooking utensils sit in a rounded pot next to the knives, which are also labeled. Decor and organization were always part of Skye's talent. I never understood why she focused her time on content creation and writing when she could have had her own interior design business, but that wasn't for me to decide.

As I gathered all the necessities for our Christmas meal, I watched her examine the box I gave her. She rubs her fingers across the top before opening it. I hear her gasp, and shortly after, she's gazing at me with those soft eyes. They turn me into mush whenever they land on me. *I wonder if she knows.*

I knew I couldn't come over empty-handed when I got her text. The movie was purchased way before our breakup. Every year, it played on the TV less and less, so I decided to buy it for her. Being able to hand it over to her has me feeling blessed, blessed I'm getting the chance to be around her again, to feel her energy.

"Want me to come help you in the kitchen?" She asks.

"I know damn well you don't like cooking…unless you be cooking for your new man."

She smirks and says, "Yeah, I don't cook for him either," then focuses back on the movie. Although she's laughing, I can tell it's fake, but I won't pry.

"How do you survive? I know your little ass likes to eat," I say, trying to lighten the mood.

"That's what I have Emily for. She feeds me, and I keep her in business."

"Dynamic Duo."

"Today, you'll have to take her place," she says, grabbing her blanket and snuggling up.

Skye fell asleep on the couch in the middle of the movie and my cooking. I notice how peaceful she looks when I approach her, and even though I'm ready to eat, I don't want to disturb her sleep, but that changes when we hear a loud knock on the door.

"Why are you in my face?" She blushes. "Were you watching me the entire time?"

"Do you think I'm a creep?" I ask with a smirk. She laughs, and I continue, "I came to wake you up. The food is ready."

"Smells good," she says, wiping her eyes.

Another knock on the door rushes her up. "I'm coming."

"Were you expecting anyone?"

"No, I was supposed to be at my aunt's house," she says, opening the door.

"Should I go?"

~

Skye

I should have looked before opening the door, but I wasn't thinking. Since I hadn't spoken to him in a week, I wasn't expecting to see him at my doorstep. I watched as his gaze shifted from me and landed on Desmond.

"Should I go?" Desmond asks.

I still haven't told anyone we aren't together, so I'm sure Desmond thinks he might be overstepping by being here. I appreciate him wanting to give us the space to talk, but I'm good. There's not much left for me to say to Lance.

"You probably should," Lance says, entering my apartment without being invited in. Way too comfortable for me. I can't believe he has the balls.

"It was nice seeing you, Skye," Desmond says, walking to the door.

Taking hold of his wrist, I pull him back towards me. "No, you're my guest, and you're staying. We haven't eaten."

I don't care how it looks to Lance. He has no right to barge into my apartment and tell my company to leave. Anything he has to say, he can say in front of Desmond. I'm not the one who broke things off, and I'm not the one who cut communication. Now, he shows up at my door like everything is

okay like he didn't tell me to abort the baby
he allegedly was so excited to be having.

"You sure?" Desmond asks.

"I'm more than sure. Make our plates.
This won't be long."

"You move quick. I ain't expect you to be
back with that nigga already." Lance points
at Desmond, burning a hole through him.

"You left *me*, Lance. You told me it was
over. You told me to get rid of my fucking
baby."

"So you went and ran to that nigga?"
Lance shoots daggers at Desmond.

"Maybe I should go," Desmond says,
standing in the kitchen.

"Yes," Lance responds.

"No," I shout at the same time.

"I knew you were still fucking him. I
knew it." Lance paces back and forth. "I
should have known not to get involved
with you, especially after you let me hit the
first night."

"Bro, you need to chill out with the
disrespect. I don't give a fuck how mad you
are. Get them emotions in check when it

comes to this one." Desmond glances at me. "You not about to disrespect the woman I spent four years loving." Desmond steps to Lance. "I didn't know the two of you broke up. I'm here because despite what happened between us in the past, she needed a friend, and nigga, you ain't it."

"I don't believe that shit. Not too long ago, I caught you coming out of her place. Remember that?"

"And nothing happened, but I see you one of them insecure niggas."

Lance steps closer to Desmond. The tension is high. I love how Desmond is coming to my defense, but I do not need these men tussling in my little ole apartment, as my mom referred to it. I push my hands between them, trying to keep them separated.

"Desmond, you don't have to explain yourself. As a matter of fact, can you go to my room, please, while I talk to my *ex*," I emphasize.

Before going to my room, he glances at Lance and then back to me. "Are you going to be fine?"

I nod my head, and he walks away.

"Lance, why are you here? Actually, how did you know I was home?"

"I saw your car parked out front, and I knew you were supposed to be with your family."

"You know that's some stalker shit, right? Why are you driving by my apartment on Christmas Day? You should be with your mom."

"I was worried about you," he says, ignoring my questions."

Bullshit!

"Have you heard of a phone? If you were so worried, you could have called first. Then *this*," I point between us, "could have been avoided."

I pull out my phone to see if I happened to miss a text or call from him. I should block his ass, and if I weren't pregnant, I would. What the hell is he doing? Driving by my apartment every time he isn't at work or his mother's house? It's weird.

"I know how it sounds. It's wild and stalkerish, but I promise I was just thinking about you and wanted to see you. I miss you," he says, taking hold of my hand. "I know what I said to you was fucked up, but put yourself in my shoes. You would have thought I was cheating, same as I did."

"And it took my ex telling you he didn't fuck me to believe it?"

"Well, yeah."

"Do you know how fucked up that sounds?"

"I said I'm sorry. What else do you want from me? Want me to get on my fucking knees and beg for forgiveness."

"That's a start, but what I really want is for you to turn your ass around and walk out the door."

"Skye..."

"Lance, there is no us. There was never supposed to be an *us*," I repeat his words back to him. "Those are the words *you* said, remember?" I poke him in the chest.

"What about the baby?" I couldn't believe he was asking me this shit.

"It's my choice, remember? I'll let you know what I decide. You can go."

"I love you."

"Goodbye, Lance."

He stares at me one more time before walking out the door. I want to cry. Not because I miss him. Not because I'm in love with him. I want to cry because I'm pissed off. I want to cry because he tried to turn my words around on me. I want to cry because Desmond had to be here to witness this bullshit, to see me argue with a man I left him for—a man who has left me with a piece of him, half of him.

I can't cry, not while he's here.

"Let's eat," I yell out to Desmond, attempting to hide the pain in my voice, but he's already standing behind me when I turn around. He pulls me into a hug my heart is aching for. A hug he shouldn't want to give to me, but he does. He doesn't say a word. He holds me until I finally break down in his arms.

~

Desmond

I hadn't witnessed Skye cry like this since we lost our baby. Holding her in my arms the way I am today is how I should have held her when she was mourning the loss of a child.

I didn't fully trust her ex, so I stayed close and heard everything. I couldn't believe the shit that was coming out of that man's mouth. Skye wanted nothing more than to be a mother, and he was trying to take that away from her because of his insecurity. She hadn't even noticed me slip the note I had given her into my back pocket, and I'm glad I did. I wrote her something like a love letter, confessing how much I still loved her, but after witnessing what I did, she didn't need me in the way causing any more hurt or confusion. Whatever I need to say I'll tell it to her face when the time is right. Today wasn't that day.

I can see she's in pain, and she's trying
her hardest to conceal it, but I've studied
her long enough to know that's the face of a
woman who's been hurt enough. As much
as I want her to confide in me, to unburden
herself and put all the weight on me, I won't
force it. I'm probably the last person she
wants to lean on, but I'm not going
anywhere until I know she's good. I'll stick
around as a friend, someone she can sit with
in silence, someone she can hug and use as
a tissue to cry on.

I want to be for her what I couldn't be in
the past—present.

23
Happy New Year

Saturday, January 1, 2011

Skye

My resolution for the New Year is to stay true to myself no matter what. I want to focus on loving myself more, not caring what people think of me and my choices. I want to start taking my business more seriously than I have in the past few months.

I need to get back to Skye Ayla Rose.

I've always wondered why my mom chose that name. I have a love-hate relationship with it. But the other night, a long-forgotten memory resurfaced as I sat in my room brainstorming baby names, and suddenly, it took on a new meaning—the beauty of the world around us—the sky, the moon, and the roses.

I vividly recall the night I spent with my grandmother before she passed away. The moon was shining so bright that it lit up the entire sky. It was a sight like no other. As we sat there, my grandmother shared a memory of my mother. She reminisced about how she would spend hours lying in the driveway at night with her blankets, gazing up at the sky. My grandmother asked her what was so captivating up there, and my mother replied that she would never feel lost as long as she could see the sky and the moon. It made me wonder if my name had anything to do with it. Maybe my mother hoped that having me around would keep her from losing herself. I wondered if becoming a mother would do the same for me.

Still stuck with deciding if a mother is what I'll ever be, I chose to celebrate New Year's Eve alone. I enjoyed some apple cider, music, and chocolate chip cookies until it was time for the countdown. Emily offered to bring in the year with me when I finally told her what went down between Desmond and Lance on Christmas, but I didn't want to burden her with my drama. I

wanted her to make memories with
her fiancé.

Sitting up in bed, I finally decided to
pick up my phone. My phone buzzed
continuously with messages, but my heart
only yearned to respond to one person.

> ***Emily:*** *Happy New Year, Bestie. I love you.
> Brunch soon!*

> ***Mom:*** *Happy New Year, my Skye. I'm
> sorry. Dad and I love and miss you.*

> ***Lance:*** *Miss you, and Happy New Year*

> ***Mrs. Evans:*** *Good morning and Happy
> New Year to you and my growing
> grandbaby. May your year be filled with
> love and blessings.*

> ***Desmond:*** *Hey big head. I was texting to
> wish you a happy new year. Don't get too
> hyped up on that cider :).*

Desmond had been texting me daily
since he left me on Christmas, and I had yet
to respond. I wanted to erase the memory of
our last encounter from my mind, but it
lingered stubbornly, refusing to be

forgotten. I wish I had the courage to thank him for being there for me, for holding me tightly as I wept, but my pride held me back, worried about how he felt or what he thought of me. The way everything played out was embarrassing.

What I do want is for Lance and his mom to stop reaching out to me. I know she means no harm, but it's got to stop. All of Lance's texts are about how much he misses me, but he makes sure to never mention the baby. On the other hand, his mother can't stop mentioning her unborn grandchild. I bet he hasn't told her that he doesn't want me to see the pregnancy through, but he was so quick to tell her he would be a father when I specifically told him not to.

I'd love to talk to my mom and figure out how we can fix our mother-daughter relationship, but her words truly hurt me. She took a shot at my heart and only missed it by an inch. I've been trying to convince myself that she loves me, but I wonder if she wishes I never existed. It would explain why she's so rude to me. I'm not completely cutting her out of my life, she gave me one, but something's gotta give. Perhaps this will be the year we come together—no drama, just love.

~

Lance

"Mama, I think I fucked up."

"First, watch your mouth."

"Sorry."

"Second, you still haven't told me Happy New Year while you're sitting up here eating up my food."

"Sorry, Ma. Happy New Year."

"Thank you. Now, tell me, what the hell did you do?" She asks, sitting down at the table.

I slide my plate of black-eyed peas, rice, and fried chicken away from me. This is about to be one complicated conversation, but I can't avoid it any longer. I don't want to hurt her, nor do I want to shatter her dreams of being a grandma, but I need to be honest—with her and myself, especially after she told me she'd been texting Skye.

She started feeling like she did something wrong when Skye stopped responding to her.

I was hoping Skye had been missing me the way I missed her. I wanted another chance to work on us. It was the main reason I showed up at her place. I didn't know she'd actually be there when I showed up, but I wasn't expecting to see her ex with her in matching sweaters. Fucking matching sweaters like they were a got damn couple. Then she refused to let the man leave so I could talk to her. The way she took hold of his wrist told me everything I needed to know. But what blew me was how she threw my words back in my face like a bomb waiting to explode. I've tried reaching out to her, but she refuses to text back.

"I broke up with Skye…"

"And…"

"And told her she couldn't keep the baby."

My mom slaps me in the face so fucking hard that I almost react. I knew she'd respond similarly to me telling her the news, but damn that shit hurt. I just didn't think she'd be this upset. She puts her hand up to hit me again, and I flinch. She backs up and bursts into tears. I fucked up.

"She'll never forgive you. Even if she keeps that baby, she will never get over those words and never trust you again. How could you do that to her?" She cries.

"Mom," I say, embracing her, but she pushes me away. It reminds me of how Skye reacted when I broke up with her. "Her heart belongs to someone else. She doesn't love me. She's in love with him. I can tell from the way she looks at him and the way she speaks his name. She will never fully be mine."

"And now you'll never know." She storms to the backyard. I pissed her off. When she needs to calm down, she always goes out back to swing on her chair. "You are so wrong," she says as I follow her.

"So, how do I make it right?" I ask, sitting beside her.

"I'm not Skye. I'm not carrying your child. I don't know how she feels, but if your father had told me to get rid of my child, I would have whooped his ass and then moved out to raise you by my damn self."

"Damn."

"Yeah, damn. You a got damn fool. I know I ain't raise you to be that got damn ignorant. You better pray she keeps my grandbaby, or you'll be begging for my forgiveness, too," she says, pushing me off the swinging chair. "Now, get the hell away from me so I can relax. Up over here ruining the start to my new year with your bullshit."

24
The Final Goodbye

Skye

What a fucked-up way to start a new year. I've prayed morning, noon, and night and finally decided what to do about the baby slowly growing inside me. I confided in my best friend, my mother, and *his* mother. All of which gave me great advice.

Communicating with Lance's mother was difficult. She had lost her husband and was eagerly looking forward to becoming a grandmother, so she was more than disappointed when she found out what her son asked of me. She prayed for me to see the pregnancy through—perhaps have a son who could carry on his father's last name. I felt for her, but I had to be truthful and prioritize myself. Thankfully, she understood where I was coming from. It lifted some of the stress I'd been carrying. She asked me to promise to keep in touch, and as much as I would love to, I can't commit to that. There's no telling what kind of relationship Lance and I will have after this is done. We may never speak again.

The conversation I had with my mom went better than I expected. Despite our argument, we were able to have a civilized conversation. She cried, confused as to why I hadn't come to her in the beginning. Usually, the first person a woman goes to about her pregnancy is her mother, but after she said those horrible things to me on Christmas, I wasn't sure I wanted to come to her for advice regarding the matter. She hurt me, and it was a shame she didn't comprehend how her words and actions constantly felt like a knife to the heart. It feels like she's always finding ways to shut me out of her life, even if it's not intentional. Despite that, I needed the woman who once adored everything about me. I was feeling lost. I might not always admit it to myself, but I miss my mom.

I hadn't been aware that she suffered multiple miscarriages before having me and contemplated having an abortion when she found out she was pregnant again. The choice to voluntarily let me go seemed better than miscarrying. After speaking with my grandmother, her mind changed. My grandmother told her the third time around was the charm and that I would be just fine. Her main focus was making sure I'd be okay with the possibility of not being able to have a child if I went through with the abortion. I knew this pregnancy could be my last chance to be a mother, so I sat with that fact for a while.

Ultimately, the decision was mine and mine only, but I wanted to speak to Lance again before I scheduled anything with my doctor. I ignored him for a while, listened to countless apologies he left on my voicemail, and accepted dozens of flowers he had sent to my door. Once I stopped going back and forth on whether I should go through with the abortion, I called him.

I was relieved knowing his mind hadn't changed. I didn't need him trying to talk me out of my decision. Lance was sure he

didn't want to bring a child into a broken
family, and I respected that. Having to deal
with moving our kid back and forth from
my place to his, splitting birthdays, and
switching off holidays every year wasn't
ideal. Knowing that arguments were bound
to happen no matter how well we co-parent
with one another was another possible
issue.

I didn't want that life either.

Lance: I'm at the door.

Skye: Be there in a second. It's unlocked.

After the procedure, I'll need someone to
drive me home safely. Lance stepped up
and offered to accompany me. I was
initially surprised, especially since he
decided it was okay to disrespect me after
realizing I still had feelings for Desmond.

Before leaving my apartment, I take a
moment to look in the mirror. As I rub my
stomach, I can't help but feel a sense of guilt
for the difficult decision I've made. I pray
for forgiveness and ask for a blessing to be

bestowed upon me when the time is right—
a chance to bring new life into the world
and make up for the difficult choice to
remove life from my womb.

With a heavy heart, I turn off the light,
grab my hoodie from the bed, and head
outside with Lance.

~

The car stops, and I realize we're at my
doctor's office. I had expressed my lack of
trust in any other medical professional to
carry out the procedure, so my doctor
rearranged her schedule to accommodate
me. I ended up finding an extraordinary
black woman to be my doctor when I had
planned to see the pregnancy through. She
was kind, and I didn't feel judged when I
returned to her to say I wasn't ready for
motherhood.

"Do you want me to come in?" It was the
first sentence he had spoken to me since
getting in the car.

"I got it from here." I reach for the door but stop and look at him. "Unless you want to."

Unbuckling his seat belt, he exits the car, walks to the side, and opens my door. Holding out his hand, he asks, "Are you ready?"

"Are you?" I ask, taking hold of his hand.

"Skye, I'm here for you. I want you to be happy. I want nothing but the best for you. I don't think I'm it. You have so much to achieve. Becoming a mother isn't on the list yet, but I promise one day you will get there with the one for you. I don't want you to worry about me. I'll be alright."

"Thank you. It's a relief to hear."

"Can I ask you something before we go in?"

"Sure," I reply, preparing myself for the worst.

"When this is over and done with," he pauses, and his eyes shift to the ground, "are you going to go back to him?"

I didn't see this coming—my ex asking me about my other ex. It's not something I've thought about. Not recently, at least.

I loved Desmond.

I still love Desmond, but my decision has nothing to do with him. It's been a while since we've spoken. Breaking down in his arms over what Lance and I were going through was embarrassing. Even though I didn't disclose the details of my strained relationship with Lance, I knew Desmond figured out what was happening. When he left my house, I also noticed the letter I had left sitting on the side table by my couch was gone. Whatever he wanted to tell me, my situation made him take it back.

"That's hard to answer," I admit, getting out of the car. "Our relationship got complicated, and we honestly never got around to talking about it. It's not something I can say I'd jump back into. I need to focus on me."

"I can respect that," he says, taking me inside.

Lance and I emerge from the medical facility, our minds racing with the events that had just taken place. The procedure I had just undergone left me feeling out of sorts. Emotions run high as we silently make our way back to my place, neither of us willing to break the uneasy silence that has settled between us. I struggle to find the right words to say, but in the end, I close my eyes and try to process everything that has transpired.

As we approach my place, Lance offers to keep me company. While I appreciate his thoughtfulness, I want time alone to sort through my thoughts and emotions, so I respectfully decline his offer.

"Let me at least walk you to the door," he says, getting out of the car before I can protest.

Standing by the car still, tears stream down my face. I can't help but wonder why I'm so emotional. We both agreed to this, but as Lance walks me to the door, I feel like my life is ending. My legs are weak and shaky, making me feel grateful he didn't respect my wishes.

Despite my efforts to hide my feelings, Lance can tell I'm distraught. I don't want him to worry. I don't want him to try to fix us. I try my best to compose myself, but the tears keep falling.

"You're going to be alright." He wipes the tears from my face.

As we say our final goodbyes, Lance kisses my forehead and whispers goodbye in my ear. Our relationship has officially come to an end.

<u>25</u>

No Regrets

Thursday, January 13, 2011

Lance

Walking away from Skye was the last thing I wanted to do, but I had no right to force myself into her place, knowing I was the reason she went through with the abortion.

Honestly, I had doubts about her commitment to our relationship, but when she told me she was pregnant, I held onto the belief that we could make our situation work. She would have been a fantastic mother. I pictured her nurturing and caring for our child with unconditional love. Skye made everyone feel loved and appreciated, and I knew our child would be cared for in the same manner my mom cared for me.

All that changed when I saw her with her ex.

I knew a one-sided love wouldn't last, and I wasn't willing to fight for it.

I planted a seed in her mind that I knew she wouldn't be able to ignore, and I did it all because I wasn't man enough to put my pride to the side. I had no faith in us. I didn't even try to hear her out or see if her unresolved feelings for him were something she'd be able to let go of. Instead, I turned into those men I despise—not ready to step back up to the plate after hitting a home run, finding a way out of a situation when shit doesn't go the way they want.

That was some petty ass shit, I think, as I sit the controller down and lean back in my recliner. *I told her not to have a baby because I knew she'd end up raising it with the next man.* Sure, I would have been around, but everything in me knew that he would be a constant in our child's life, which also meant he'd be a constant in mine. Ain't no way I could look that nigga in his face every other week—smile in his face when a special occasion came around knowing I don't like his ass. So what if I don't know him like that?

Skye and Desmond let each other go once, and I doubt they'll let that kind of love slip away again. She told me she's not about to get back with him, but that's a damn lie. She might not see it happening, but my gut tells me they'll be back in each other's arms sooner than later.

I know two people in love when I see it, and they have nothing but love for each other. Their connection goes deep. I could tell by how they looked at each other the day I came to check on her and how he came to her defense when I was being an asshole. He was about ready to beat my ass if I said one more disrespectful thing to her.

She'd be much happier raising a child they created together—out of pure love.

Yeah, fuck it. I told her to do the right thing, even if my mom thinks I fucked up. There's nothing I can do about it now.

<u>26</u>

Release

Saturday, February 5, 2011

Skye

"Skye, please open the door. I know you're in there. Open up. I've been worried about you."

I hear Emily at my door, banging like a crazy woman. I appreciate her coming by to check in, but I want her to go away. I haven't been feeling like myself since the abortion. I feel like an empty shell and want to be left alone. I hadn't expected to feel like I had done something wrong, overwhelmed with guilt, and for what? Why should I feel guilty for choosing me?

"You know I have a key, right?" Emily shouts, tapping at the door impatiently. "It's almost been a month since I've seen you, so if you don't open up so I can see you're okay, I'm going to let myself in."

How could I forget I gave that bitch a key? It was only meant for emergencies, which I guess this situation could be considered one. I'm surprised she hasn't used it. "I'm coming."

Before I can reach the door, Emily is already letting herself in. She has a takeout bag in her hand—food from her restaurant that smells oh-so-good. I've been starving myself, not on purpose, but my appetite isn't what it used to be. My cravings disappeared immediately, letting me know I no longer had a human growing inside me.

"I love you," Emily says, wrapping her arms around me.

"I love you too," I say, embracing her. "Sorry I haven't been picking up your calls or responding to your text. I've just been trying to get back to myself."

"And that's why I'm here. I know you wanted to handle this alone, but you need someone to lean on, laugh with...cry if needed. You made a huge decision, and I need to know you're doing alright."

"I promise I'm fine."

"Skye, you can't lie to me. I can tell by this dark-ass room, those sweatpants, and the mess on top of your head that you aren't. It's okay to admit you're hurting."

I couldn't get a lie past Emily for the life of me. She always knows when something is up, but she's right—I'm not. I'm lonely and depressed, but I couldn't and wouldn't allow anyone to see me in this state. I haven't showered in days. My hair hasn't been washed in weeks, and my apartment looks run-through.

"I'm not myself, but I'll be fine…I'm just going through the motions. Some days, I feel okay, but most of the time I feel nothing at all."

"Have you been working?"

I hadn't. I didn't want to see anyone and wasn't ready to take on any more clients. "I need to get myself together before I go back."

"Going back will get you together. It's not like you have to leave the house to get some of your work done. The quicker you return to your routine, the sooner you'll start to heal."

"Heal from what?" I roll my eyes.

"From the failed relationship," Emily pauses, "from…the abortion."

She didn't want to say it, but I needed to hear it. I needed someone to acknowledge that I had made a life-changing decision. I needed someone to help me realize that what I went through was real and not a figment of my imagination. I had the life sucked from me literally, and even though I did it for me, for my sanity, it was the one thing that was driving me to a dark empty place. I had always wanted to bring life into this world, but not into a broken relationship, not when the father wasn't willing to co-parent in that type of situation.

Lance and I haven't spoken since he dropped me off. After our final goodbye, he completely ghosted. I didn't understand how it could be so easy for him to disappear from my life as if we had never existed as one.

"It had to happen. I know it did. I don't understand this emptiness. It's scary, Em. I want *me* back. I want to smile again, and I want to love again." I start crying.

"Let it out. I'm here for you." Emily wraps her arms around me like a mother. I could use mine by my side, but I wasn't willing to let myself be more vulnerable than I had already been.

I cried in Emily's arms until I couldn't cry anymore. Wiping my face dry, she sat me at the table, placing the food she'd brought in front of me, forcing me to eat something. While I ate, Emily turned on the music and tidied up my apartment. It felt like waking up on a Saturday morning as a child. Opening the blinds and windows to let in light and fresh air, something I hadn't had in weeks, caused me to adjust my eyes and slowly breathe.

Once I finished eating, Emily ran me a bath with all of my favorite products. She washed my body and hair, then instructed me to shower when we were done. My best friend was providing me the peace and care

I had been refusing from everyone for
weeks.

"Thank you." I turn to her. "Thank you
for coming to check in on me. For being the
best friend I could ever ask for."

"I'm here for you whenever you need
me. Next time you take this long to speak to
me, I'm kicking in the door."

"But you have a key." I laugh.

"You need to know how serious this is.
Fuck that key." She chuckles. "I love you,
Skye Ayla Rose."

"I love you too, Emily Ray Foster."

"We haven't walked down the aisle
yet…but his last name does sound good
with mine." Emily blushes.

<u>27</u>
Valentine's Day

Monday, February 14, 2011

Skye

Emily's restaurant is giving off all the vibes. It's almost drowning in red and white roses, teddy bear toppers, and heart balloons. It screams, Happy Valentine's Day. Today is either one you love or hate. It isn't everyone's cup of tea, but walking in here will give one an involuntary love high.

I was reluctant to come and nearly walked back into my place, but I needed to leave my apartment and enjoy the company of human beings. I started back work, but I've been craving real human interaction. Coming here is precisely how I'm going to get it.

Emily's spot has never been this lit, especially on a Monday, but it's a day to celebrate the people you love, including yourself. I see the drinks flowing as people dance to the music played by the DJ she hired—a beautiful sight. It warms my heart.

Toward the back, Emily has us a designated booth, secluded from the busy crowd.

"Over here," I hear her announce as I walk through the restaurant.

I wave, but my hand freezes when I see him. That man still makes my heart jump out of my chest, and my pussy drips at the sight of him.

This can't be Desmond Walker, not the Desmond who refused to grow a beard or let his hair grow the whole time we were together. I guess men change their appearance like women after a breakup. I overlooked the glow-up when I was buying all those damn pregnancy tests. I was too busy trying to become invisible.

In the time I haven't seen him, his hair has grown out more and is braided to the back, stopping just below his ears. His face is covered in a sexy-ass goatee and full beard. When he smiles, the diamond grill at the bottom of his teeth gleams. If I didn't have any sense, I'd hop right in his lap and get to work.

Is it possible to develop muscles like that in two months? I feel like I haven't seen him in years.

"It's been a while," Jordan says once I approach them.

"Yeah, we've missed you," Desmond says, standing up.

"I missed you…I mean, I missed you all too." Emily looks at me and smirks while Desmond cracks up.

"Sit here," Desmond says, allowing me to scoot beside Emily. I'm sandwiched between them, but I'm not complaining. I haven't been next to a man in months, and being next to one as fine as him is a godsend.

"You look nice today," he says, wrapping the curl hanging loose in front of my face around his finger and then letting it go.

I wore a bright red jumpsuit that hung off my shoulders and came down into a v-cut. I taped my breasts so they would look fuller than they were. The jumpsuit flared out at the bottom, and I wore pink high-heels to make me appear taller. The main issue I had when it came to a good jumpsuit was my height. They always hung to the floor, showing how tiny I indeed was.

"Today?" I narrow my eyes.

"I mean… you always look sexy, but I haven't seen you in months."

"Yeah, about that…."

"No need to explain." He smiles at me, almost taking an eye out from the brightness of his grill.

"What are we drinking?" I need one. Being next to him is getting me hot and bothered.

"Are you allowed to drink… you know, with everything going on?" Desmond whispers in my ear.

I guess Emily does know how to keep a secret. I thought she would have told Jordan about my decision, and he definitely would have told Desmond.

"I decided I wasn't ready to take that step."

He plants his hand on my thigh and says, "I'm so sorry."

I can tell he is being genuine. Most men would have been delighted that the woman they loved gave up another man's child, but not Desmond. I can see he is concerned, but he doesn't know I made it through the challenging part thanks to Emily's help.

"No need to be sorry." I place my hand on top of his and squeeze. I swear I feel a shock wave throughout my body. He must have sensed it, too, because our eyes instantly lock, and we snatch our hands from one another. "When the time is truly right for me, I'll have everything I want with the person I need."

"Let's drink up then," he says, squeezing my thigh.

After more than a few drinks and plenty of French toast and bacon, I stood on the chair dancing like my life depended on it. The restaurant had closed to the rest of the public, and it was just the four of us and the staff. I hadn't had this much freedom in what seemed like a lifetime, and I was enjoying every moment. Jordan and Emily shook their heads and grinned as I sang "What's My Name" by Rihanna.

"What's her name, Des?" Jordan jokes.

"Yeah, say her name," Emily instigates.

"Say my name," I say, leaning down to whisper in his ear.

"Is he gonna say it?" Emily giggles.

"Nah, he's not gonna say it," Jordan answers her.

"Skye," he says, tickling me down into his lap. "Skye needs to sit her drunk ass down." He chuckles as I try to get out of his grasp.

"Which one of you is taking her drunk ass back home?" He sits me up. "Did you drive?"

Pulling out my keys, I jingle them in Desmond's face. "How else do you think I got here?"

"OK, smart-ass. I'll drive you back home and walk to my place once I know you're fine."

"But I'm not ready to leave yet."

"He's right, Skye. You haven't drunk in months, and if you have one more drink, my staff is going to be picking you up off the floor, and I'll have to pay them for overtime."

"But, who's going to drive your car?" I ask Desmond.

"He rode with me," Jordan intervenes. "Let the man get you home safe. We can plan a night out since you missed him…I mean…*us*, so much." He chuckles.

"Oh, shut up. That was a slip of the tongue."

"So you haven't missed me?" Desmond tries to read my face for an answer.

"I'm not saying that."

"So you have?" He drapes his arm around my shoulder.

"I'm not saying that either."

"Then what are you saying?"

"She misses you," Emily cuts us off, "Now could you please take her home before she gets to standing on my shit again."

"I love you guys," I say, pulling Emily into me. "I love you sooooo much."

"I love you too, but let me go."

"NO. I want to stay," I whine.

Pulling me by the waist, Desmond throws me over his shoulder and grabs my purse. "I'll text J when I get her home."

"Thank you so much, Desmond. You're a lifesaver." Emily hugs Desmond goodbye and then locks the door behind us. She and Jordan have some cleaning to do.

~

Desmond

As soon as I get Skye into the car, her eyes struggle to stay open. She strokes the side of her temples, which only means her world is probably spinning from all the vodka she's ingested. When we approach our neighborhood, she begs me to hurry and get her out of the car, causing me to speed up.

"I need to throw up," she declares as I park.

Snatching her up, I run to her door, unlock it, and rush her to the bathroom. As soon as she lifts the toilet, she throws up her insides for at least thirty minutes. Once she finishes, she brushes her teeth and crawls to the bed. It was only 6:00 p.m., and the sun was still out, but Skye was done.

"Are you able to take a shower?"

"I can try," she whispers.

Picking out her sleepwear, I help her undress, but not before asking for permission. I've watched her struggle to remove her clothes while drunk plenty of times, and it was never a pretty sight. Once she is undressed, I quickly place a towel around her before my eyes stray to places I'm forbidden to touch.

"How does that feel?" I ask once I place her in the shower, still looking away from the art before me.

"It's not hot enough."

Turning the knob a bit more, I hear a moan escape her lips. "That's better," she says, exhaling.

"Um, I'll be in the living room," I say with my back turned. "Your change of clothes is on the bed. Scream if you need me."

"Thank you, Des," she says softly.

"Anytime."

Sitting on the couch, I rest my eyes before I realize an hour has passed. No sound is coming from Skye's room, so I jump up to make sure she hasn't fallen in the shower or some shit. When I enter her room, she's sleeping peacefully, still wrapped in her towel. I admire her beauty and thank God for allowing me to witness it again.

I guess I can make my way home.

Leaning down, I plant a kiss on her forehead. "Good night and sweet dreams, my beautiful Skye."

Pulling away, I feel her soft hand wrap around my wrist. "Hold me, please," she asks sweetly, eyes still partially closed.

"Is that what you want?"

"It's what I need."

I remove my shoes and climb into bed beside her. Wrapping my arms over her body, she snuggles closer to me. I inhale her lavender and vanilla scent and drift off to sleep.

<u>28</u>

Images of You

Tuesday, February 15, 2011

Skye

The weight of his arm is no longer there. I can't feel his body pressed against mine. *Was it all a dream? Is my imagination playing with me?*

It couldn't have been a dream. I'm still in the towel I fell asleep in, but the man I remember asking to stay is nowhere to be found. I know he was here because I still smell him on my pillow. The spot next to me is still warm. *Maybe he didn't want to wake me when he went home.*

Rolling on my back, I unwrap my towel, visualizing Desmond beside me still—his fingers gradually gliding up my thighs. My center is already moist from the thought of Desmond circling my clit with his tongue. Smearing my juices over my lower lips, I massage my clit, sending vibrations through me as I take my free hand to massage my breast. The more I envision Desmond, the more pressure builds inside me. I hear my moans echo throughout the bedroom. I arch my back off the bed, and a rush goes through me. Moving my fingers down, I enter myself slowly, bucking against them as if this is the last orgasm I'll be allowed to have.

"Fuck," I cry out as my juices coat my fingers.

Withdrawing my hand from my breast. I rub my clit in a circular motion as I continue to tease my insides.

"Desmond," I moan with my eyes closed, "I miss you."

"I miss you too," I hear a deep raspy voice.

I open my eyes to see Desmond standing in my doorway with coffee from the cafe around the corner in his hands.

"Fuck," I yell out, but I can't stop my fingers from devouring my insides.

I'm on the verge of another orgasm and can't stop now. I need the release, and I don't care if he is watching me get it. He'd been watching for this long—a few more minutes wouldn't kill him.

"Should I go?" He turns away, sitting my coffee on the TV stand.

My mind is screaming yes, but my body is communicating the opposite.

"Turn back around," I demand, "I'm coming again."

"Are you sure?"

"It's nothing you haven't seen before," I say before another moan escapes my lips.

As Desmond turns back to face me, I spread my legs wide, giving him a full view of my glistening pussy. I remove the fingers I'd been using to please myself and rub them around my lips. Looking at him with hunger, I place them in my mouth, imagining they're his dick. I can feel myself leaking as I continue to suck on them. I take them out and insert them back into my pussy one at a time, never taking my gaze off Desmond.

"Damn, that feels good," I moan.

"Skye."

"Desmond."

"You gotta stop."

"Why?" I ask faintly.

"Because if I have to watch you have one more orgasm, my balls are going to turn blue."

"Then let me fuck you until they feel better," I plead.

"I can't let you do that."

"And why not?" I say, stopping my movements.

"Because I love you too much to fuck you and then walk away. If I lay next to you right now, fucking is the last thing on my mind. I want to make love to you, and if I do that, I'm going to want to for the rest of our lives. I don't know if you're willing to spend a lifetime getting this love."

Pulling the blanket from the edge of my bed, I cover myself. I suddenly feel dirty and dismissed. I run into the bathroom, closing the door behind me. I can't look at Desmond after what I've just done.

"Stupid. I'm so fucking stupid for thinking we could go back to normal."

"You're not stupid," I hear Desmond say. "You're smart and sexy as fuck. Please don't be embarrassed or feel rejected."

"How can I not be embarrassed?" I ask, opening the door, blanket wrapped around me.

"Because it's me."

"And you just curved the hell out of me."

"I could pull out my dick and give you what you want right here, right now, but what would that do?"

"Make me cum, the way you used to beg me to."

"And then what?"

"And…and then—"

"And then you don't know," he says, grabbing my chin. "If I go there with you, I promise you, you won't be able to get rid of me. If you want to take it there, we can do that, but I think we have a few things to discuss before that occurs."

"Like what?" I ask.

We have a lot to talk about, but do I really want to? Not really, but I don't think he's going to give me a choice.

"Like the loss of our baby. The fucked-up way I dealt with it. How you suddenly decided you'd be better off without me. We got shit to talk about Skye Ayla Rose. Until we do that, there's no way we can have a fresh start."

"Then let's talk about it now." *Get this shit out of the way.*

"Nah, you're horny." He gazes at me. "I see it all in your eyes."

"You're right." I laugh. "Then what about this weekend?"

"Saturday?" He suggests.

"Perfect."

"Great," he says, adjusting himself. "I'm going to get out of here before I change my mind and take you up on that last offer."

~

Desmond

I let the cold water run over me as I try to get the image of Skye making love to herself out of my mind. That shit was so damn sexy to see.

We'd made love plenty of times, but she was never one to let me watch her play with herself. She has always been a little shy, so I was stunned at first. The view was immaculate, and as much as I knew I should have been looking away, my eyes were locked in. I wanted to dive in the second my name rolled off her lips as she came.

Wrapping my hand around my dick, I jerk off at the thought of that pussy squeezed tight around it.

I bet it was wet and warm as hell.

I haven't been inside another woman since Skye. Opportunities presented themselves, but I was never intrigued. I was missing how she felt and how perfectly I fit inside her. I sped up my movements, imagining Skye's tiny frame bouncing on my dick as I held on tight to her waist, one arm wrapped around her and the other massaging her clit.

Each time I envisioned her pouncing, I got closer to my release. I was rock fucking hard, and I had to get all that nut settled inside of me out.

Desmond, I miss you.

Replaying those words got me to the edge, and I felt the warm stickiness dripping on my hands and spread across my dick as I continued to rub the rest out.

We need to figure this shit out quick.

I can't go another day without her. I was okay with staying in the friend zone, but the show she put on let me know there is space for me in her world, and I refuse to let another man swoop her up again. I can't miss out on my second chance.

<u>29</u>

Our (Official) Ending

February 20, 2010

Desmond

Skye: *Are you home?*

Desmond: *I'm surprised to hear from you.*

Skye*: Are you home or not Desmond? I need to talk to you.*

Desmond*: Yeah, I'm here...Come through.*

Skye*: I'm at your door.*

Skye moved into her apartment a month ago; we haven't talked since. She told me she needed her space, and I had to respect her wishes and give it to her—despite the itch in my fingers to pick up the phone and send her a "Hey stranger" message. I'm unsure what the urgency is, but whatever she needs to discuss must be important, or she wouldn't have shown up unannounced. That's not in her character.

Easing toward the door, I clear my throat and take two deep breaths. Reaching for the doorknob, I feel my heart beating out of my chest. Once I build up the confidence to open the door, Skye is standing there with her arms across her chest and glossy eyes as if she'd been crying on her way over.

My first instinct is to wrap my arms around her, but she quickly stops me—raising a hand to halt any further movement.

"I'm not here for all that," Skye says aggressively.

"My bad. You look like you could use a hug." I raise my hands and back away from her. "Come in."

"No thanks. We can talk out here. What I have to say will be quick."

"You sure?"

"I'm positive," she responds confidently.

"Okay then," I say, closing the door behind me, "What's so important?"

"There's no easy way to say this," she hesitates, "but I think we should be done."

"What do you mean, done?"

"Just done. Let's end this," she says, annoyed.

I'm trying to comprehend what she's saying because I know she didn't come here to break up with me. Can't be no way.

"Is our break over, and we're getting back together? Because if that's the case, you don't seem thrilled about it."

"Don't play dumb, Desmond. You know what done means, but since you want me to spell it out for you, our time is up. You, me, and this relationship are done and over with," she says, turning her head away. "Our relationship has served its purpose, and I'm done. I'm not coming back."

"Who is he, Skye?" I ask, turning her head back toward me. "You must have met someone else because *this* makes no sense to me. I thought you showed up at my door because you missed me…because you were ready to come back home. Get back to us, but you on some bullshit."

"Why do you have to assume I have another man? Maybe I want to be alone. Maybe I want to take time to find myself."

"Because what other reason do you have to call it quits? We had a plan. I thought all you needed was a little space. I've given you that, so what did I do for you to want to leave me for good?"

"Plans change Desmond. I've had time to think and can't do this with you anymore. I can't allow you to sit around waiting on me."

"Stop playing with me."

"Playing," she says with a puzzling laugh.

"Yeah, playing. I'm not stupid, Skye. I got people hitting me up, saying they've seen you around town with another nigga. I know we were on a little break, but it sounds like you were out here making love connections while I've been sitting at home waiting."

"It's not like that," Skye tries convincing me.

"You know, at first, I didn't overthink it, but now you're at my doorstep telling me I've served my fucking purpose. What the fuck purpose is that?" I glare at her.

"You showed me that love is real. That it can feel like a dream come true. But you also showed me that it doesn't last forever, and relationships are bound to end. Love isn't always enough to keep a relationship going." Skye pauses as tears fall down her face.

Usually, this is the moment I'd kiss her tears dry, but there's no point. It won't change how she's feeling. I haven't stopped loving her, but I'm starting to feel like she no longer loves me.

"Just say you met someone else and want to see where it goes instead of lying about it."

"I'm sorry, and you're right…I have met someone, and I like him. He doesn't hide from me, and he doesn't avoid the hard conversations."

"Do you love him, Skye?"

"No, but I'm willing to let you go to see where he and I can go."

"Can you please come inside so we can talk about this?" I reach for her hand. I can't let us end like this.

"Desmond, I'm sorry. I have to go."

"Skye, I can't imagine life without you. You're the woman, the only woman for me. Please don't walk away from me. Don't leave me," I beg.

"Don't make this harder than it already is," Skye says, wiping the tears from her face.

"Skye," I yell after her as she walks off, "If you walk away, don't bother coming back. I won't wait for you. I'm serious."

My words mean nothing. She continues walking until she's vanished from my view. Leaving me angry and heartbroken.

<u>30</u>

Questions Answered

Saturday, February 19, 2011

Skye

Desmond picked me up around 11:00 a.m.

The night before, he instructed me to pack an overnight bag and be prepared to lay everything out on the table. If we were going to rekindle what we once had, there could be no secrets or resentment left between us. Desmond knew he wanted to be with me. There wasn't a doubt in his mind. I, on the other hand, required closure. I needed answers.

We drove down the coast, sharing very few words.

I continuously asked where we were going, but he had no intention of telling me. He insisted I be quiet and enjoy the playlist he made for me and the view. I didn't object—the sounds of cars zooming by and

the breeze accompanied by the sounds
of 90s R&B were soothing. Almost three
hours later, I woke up in front of a beautiful
house surrounded by water and trees. If I
hadn't known better, I would have thought
Desmond brought me here to murder and
dispose of my body.

"How did you find this place, and why
have you never brought me here?" I ask,
exiting Desmond's black Jeep Wrangler.

"It's been on my list of places to visit for
a while, but we never got the chance," he
says, unloading our bags and a giant cooler
that I hadn't noticed. I could tell we would
be tucked inside for the whole weekend.

"Well, it's breathtaking," I reply, taking
in the scenery.

The house sat high on the bluff and had
a 180-degree oceanfront view. We had to be
sitting on an acre of land.

"Where are we exactly?"

"Why? You think I'm going to kill you?"
He stops and winks at me.

"You know what's funny?" I grin and look down. "The thought crossed my mind as soon as I opened my eyes."

"The one thing I'll never do is hurt you," he pauses, "but I might have to end the next man that thinks he's going to take my spot." He smirks, taking our luggage inside before I can speak.

The whole time we were apart, I hadn't stopped to think that maybe, just maybe, this man was still madly in love with me.

I sat outside for a while and took in the view. Two wooden chairs sat near the end of the lawn, close to the cliffs. I perched there, taking in the ocean's waves and the cool breeze. I wasn't ready to go inside to spill my hurt and regrets to the only man I've loved with all of me. I didn't know how to tell him that breaking up with him was the biggest mistake of my life. I made it seem like walking away was easy. It was harder than suffering through the loss of a child.

"The Sea Ranch," Desmond's voice echoes.

"Huh?"

"You asked where we are. We're in a town called The Sea Ranch," he yells and returns inside.

Fitting, I think, looking from the house back to the ocean. *It does look like a ranch next to the sea.*

~

Desmond

I watched from the door as Skye took in the Ocean view. She'd been out there for hours, and I wanted to enjoy it with her, but I knew this was time she needed to herself.

I can't say if Skye is still in love with me like I'm in love with her, but I hope she is. My world revolves around Skye. She's my sun, moon, star, and all that makes this universe. When she left me, the world turned grey—all the beauty vanished, and when I ran into her in that drugstore, all the color rushed back into my life. It was like seeing her for the first time. The only people that existed were us, but then I saw those pregnancy tests, which reminded me of how I lost her in the first place.

Would we have been okay if she hadn't had a miscarriage, or would we have drifted apart anyway?

"Can I join you?" I ask, approaching Skye.

"Is one of those sandwiches mine?" She licks her lips.

The woman could eat, and I knew she had to be hungry. I made us a BLT on a toasted French baguette.

"I'm assuming that's a yes." I pass her a plate and then sit.

"Thank you," she says, glancing at me and quickly turning away. "It's peaceful here."

I had planned to bring Skye for our third anniversary, but our world and relationship took a turn I wasn't prepared for. I spent all my time hanging out with Jordan, avoiding honest conversations. Skye moved as if nothing had happened, but she resented me. The way she looked at me had altered. She wouldn't acknowledge me some days, but I pretended to be blind to it all, assuming we'd return to normal.

"Something told me you could use some peace in your life."

"We all could," she gives me half a smile.

As I'm about to open my mouth to speak, Skye sits her plate on her lap and asks, "Why?"

"Why?" I turn my chair toward her, but she stands and rushes to the house. "Skye."

I follow her toward the house, but she closes the door before I can enter.

That took an unexpected turn.

Skye is opening the bottle of champagne I planned to drink after we came to some resolution.

"Would you like a glass?" She asks, never looking up.

"Um, do you want to explain what's happening?" I ask, setting the plates on the counter.

"Yeah, I'll pour you a glass."

Picking up her glass and leaving mine where it sat, she goes to the backyard patio.

It was apparent she cracked open a door she wasn't willing to let me walk through. She's doing everything she can to shut me out, but it's too late. I need to know what she meant, what she genuinely asked me. We've gone too long without speaking the truth—without closure. If I have to break down that door, then so be it. I don't care what's on the other side.

"Did you know there was a fire pit out here?" She says, avoiding eye contact. Instead, she's concentrating on the ocean. The sun is setting, and even though it's beautiful, I'm not here to talk about that or the damn fire pit.

"Yeah, I know," I say, sitting beside her.

"Turn it on."

"Answer my question first."

"What question?" She closes her eyes and takes a sip of her drink.

"You asked me why. Why what?"

"Nothing," she says and sighs.

"Skye."

"Yes, Desmond," she huffs.

"Look at me, please, and answer the question."

"I said it's nothing. Are you going to turn on the pit or not?"

Within a few hours of our arrival, her whole demeanor switched. When we arrived, she looked comfortable, at peace, and ready for a new beginning. Once I came back outside to check on her, her attitude changed. She didn't know how to deal with whatever was bothering her. Not wanting to start an argument, I turn on the outside fireplace and step toward the sliding door to go inside.

"So, you're just going to leave me out here?"

Freezing in place, I close the sliding door back and face Skye. She gazes at me with teary eyes and a sad expression.

"I don't know what you want from me. I can't tell if you're glad to be here or regretting coming on this trip. You said you wanted to talk, and I brought you here to talk. You ask me a vague-ass question and then refuse to elaborate."

"I-I-Never-mind." She wipes her tears and turns around.

My instinct is to go to her side, but I'm baffled.

I turn to go back into the house. If the whole weekend is going to be like this, I'm going to need more than a glass of champagne. I go into the kitchen and pull out the bottle of VSOP I brought along.

Skye can sit outside, contemplating whether she wants to speak.

Snatching up the bottle, I wander upstairs and run myself a bath. Thanks to the floor-length glass windows surrounding me, I can still see the view from the bathroom.

Slipping out my clothes, I sink into the bath. Grabbing my phone, I go to my music library and hit shuffle. "Beauty" by Dru Hill comes on. *I don't want to hear this sad-ass shit*, I think, and hit next. "Let's Start Love Over," by Miles Jaye, comes on, and for a second, I'm vibing until I hear the lyrics. It was as if my damn playlist was trying to torture me.

~

Skye

"Did he walk away from me again," I mumble before drinking my glass of champagne like its lemonade.

Is he that fucking stupid that he doesn't know why the fuck I'm asking him, "Why?" Maybe coming here was a fucking mistake and horrible judgment on my behalf because I thought I wanted him to fuck my brains out. I storm into the kitchen to seize the bottle of champagne until I hear "Deuces" by Chris Brown blasting through the house.

"Oh, and he wants to be funny," I say, bringing the bottle's opening to my mouth and downing as much as I can before storming up the steps to start an argument.

I follow the music into the enormous bathroom he's in. It's about the size of the main bedroom, and as much as I want to take in the beauty, I'm too upset to admire it.

"Deuces, huh? You want me to fucking leave?" I shout, dropping the bottle to the floor and causing it to shatter. I forgot it was in my hand.

"What the fuck, Skye?" Desmond hops up, Hennessy bottle in hand, and almost slips from the tub. "Have you lost your damn mind?"

"I'm asking you a question." I step toward him, cutting my foot on the glass. "Shit!"

Before I know it, Desmond's out of the tub. His naked ass is carrying me to the bed, dick out and covered in bubbles. Placing me on the bed, he returns to the bathroom and retrieves the first-aid kit. Getting down on one knee, he rests my foot on his upper thigh and examines the bottom like he's some fucking doctor. *I should jam my foot right up his damn nose.*

"Is there glass in there?" I ask through muffled tears.

"No. You got lucky," he says, cleaning the cut and placing a band-aid over it. "It's a little scratch."

He kisses my foot, then gets off the floor to slip on the sweatpants beside me. Here I am, being a bipolar ass bitch, and he still manages to be attentive and kind. *It's cute but annoying.*

"Why weren't you there…that night?" I break down in tears. "Why did you have to go out that night?" I stand up and hit him in the chest repeatedly. "I was alone. You left me alone and kept leaving me after."

I no longer sense my legs underneath me, and as I'm about to fall to the floor, Desmond uses all his strength to keep me up. Pulling me close, I feel drops of water coating my shoulders.

"Let me go." I try pulling away, but he refuses to loosen his grip as he cries with me in his arms.

"I'm sorry. I'm sorry I wasn't strong enough to be the man you needed." His voice breaks. "I wanted to be there for you but didn't know how."

Breaking out of his grip, I shove him back as hard as possible. "But where were you that night? Why wasn't I able to contact you the next morning?" I aggressively wipe the tears from my face.

"Skye," he frowns, "you know where I was."

"Do I?"

"I was hanging out with the guys. My phone died, and I fell asleep."

"Says every guy that cheats."

"Is that what you think? Is that why you resent me so much? Not because we lost our baby, but because you assumed I was cheating on you the night it happened?"

"Well," I say, straightening my face and standing tall.

"I'm not about to do this with you right now. You should know me better than that," he says, heading toward the door.

"There you go, leaving again." I throw my slides at the door.

Stopping, his body stiffens, and he faces me. "Do you even know what tomorrow is?" He pauses and waits for me to answer.

"Sunday," I answer. "What the fuck does that have to do with anything." I cross my arms over my chest.

"*You* left me," his voice deepens, and his nostrils flare. "On February 20th, you left me for the second time," he informs me, slamming the door behind him, leaving me stuck on stupid.

How could I forget it was coming up on a year since I broke his heart?

I've been so wrapped up in my pain that I haven't even stopped to think about what Desmond's been going through. I wouldn't have agreed to come on this trip if I remembered what this date meant for us, but I was so eager to resolve things with him so we could return to the people we once were, but the truth is we'll never be those people again.

<u>31</u>
More Questions Answered

Sunday, February 20, 2011

Desmond

I laid on an uncomfortable recliner all night, wondering if we could repair what we had broken. I hadn't planned on arguing with Skye when I decided to do this trip. Fighting and arguing never sat well with me. Being accused of shit I didn't even come close to doing always felt like a form of disrespect. I pride myself in being honest and loyal but come to find out, my woman didn't trust me, and knowing that damn near unraveled me.

Skye was unmatched. No one compared. No part of me would have jeopardized our relationship. I was making plans, looking to build a future. She should be making wedding plans along with Emily. That's how sure my love for her was and still is.

Meanwhile, she felt like I switched up on her because I was cheating. It's beyond anything words can express. I'd never been so upset.

She resented me and used that resentment to try starting over with another man. Now it makes sense why she keeps bringing up how I left her, but the truth is she was the one who wanted to go separate ways. She's the one who wanted to take a break in the first place. I only agreed, trusting that our love would bring us back together. I bet my life on us, and when she left me, I almost ended it because, without Skye, there was nothing worth living for. If Jordan had appeared at my door 5 minutes later, it would have been lights out. No one knew I had become depressed to the point of wanting to end it all.

Skye says I kept leaving her when I only wanted her to stay.

~

Skye

Last night took an unexpected turn after I accused Desmond of cheating. I never believed him when he told me he was just hanging with his friends. He was never one to stay out till the morning, and he always, and I mean *always,* answered his phone. Another woman seemed to be the only logical reason. I was starting to think I was wrong, especially after I cried my eyes out to Emily. I couldn't believe my mind had even gone there, but it did, and I had been living in that space for quite some time.

She talked to Jordan, and he remembered the night in full detail. Desmond fell asleep on his couch and forgot to charge his phone. When he woke up, he knew I was going to be pissed, but there was no way he could have known my body would have rejected our child, and there was no way he could have predicted he'd get that wasted and not make it back home. Jordan might have cleared up my cheating assumptions, but it doesn't take away the fact that he focused more on spending time with his friends than his woman in the aftermath.

All he had to do was be there. We didn't need to speak. We didn't have to cry. None of it. All I required was his presence.

I spent the rest of my night upstairs because I was too embarrassed to face Desmond after losing my shit. He left the room and never came back up. If he had anything special planned for us last night, I ruined it before he could act. Luckily, he had stocked the fridge in my room with all my favorite treats and drinks, so I munched on junk before I fell asleep.

Emily: Hey Babe! Checking in to see how you're doing. I also have some good news for you.

Skye: Good morning! Please share.

After texting back, I sat my phone down and changed into my workout clothes. A walk in nature is always the perfect reset. Throwing my hair into a bun, I wash my face and brush my teeth. Putting in my earbuds, I brace myself before opening the door.

Desmond's room is directly across from mine, and I want to avoid him at all costs. The way his voice deepened, and his face turned cold was new to me. He'd been so pleasant since reconnecting, but he was apparently still feeling a certain way. Deep down, he'd been hiding his emotions—the pain of our ending—never understanding why. He held a wave of anger that came rushing to the surface, thanks to my outburst.

Peaking around the corner before descending the stairs, I see no sign of him. The house is quiet. *I know he didn't leave me here.* I look around, but to my relief, the Jeep is still parked out front.

Scrolling through my playlist, I turn on Avril Lavigne's "Complicated" and jog in place. Taking my left ankle into my hand, I pull my leg back, stretch for 10 seconds, and switch to the next leg. Rolling my neck and body around a few times, I shake myself off and jog toward the trail in the back of the house. The breeze brushes across my face as the trees sway in the wind, and I speed up as "Stupid Little Love Song" by Fefe Dobson plays. I'm in the zone as I pump my fist and start singing. I can feel my heart pumping. I'm breathing heavily, but my playlist keeps me going. I close my eyes briefly as I let the music overtake me and run into what feels like a tree. I stumble back, but I'm wrapped in arms before I hit the pavement.

"Watch where you're—" I'm getting ready to give whoever this person is a piece of my mind until I look up and see Desmond. "Oh, hey. Thanks."

"Why are you running with your eyes closed?"

"Um," is all I can get out.

Letting me go, he says, "I'll let you finish your run."

I stop him before he gets the chance to walk away. I can't continue without us getting our feelings off our chest, and I need to apologize for accusing him of something he didn't do. I needed him to know I don't blame him for my miscarriage.

"Do you want to walk and talk?" I ask.

"I've been out here for almost two hours. I should get back and eat something."

"I'll come with you then."

"You sure?"

"I'm certain." I take hold of his hand.

It surprises me when he locks his fingers with mine, but I'm relieved he isn't as upset as I assumed. Our hands intertwined feels right, despite the tension swirling between the two of us. Butterflies flutter in my stomach when he strokes my thumb with his. I want to put moments like this in a box and lock them away forever.

~

Desmond

"I'm sorry," we say in unison.

"You first," I say, placing my fork on the plate. "I want to hear what you have to say, and this time, I won't run away."

"First, I want to apologize for throwing my house shoes at you—"

"You were angry."

"Still, I was doing too much," she says, grabbing my hand from across the table—the second time she'd done that today. She held my hand, walking back to the house, never letting go, and now, she was holding on again, tighter than before. "I know you didn't step out on me."

"But you doubted me." I pull away. "It got me thinking."

Her eyes shift from our hands and back up to me. Uncertainty and disappointment are written over her delicate face—sadness fighting to escape her eyes.

"About what?"

"Did you ever love me?"

Her beautiful brown eyes grow wide, and she smirks.

"Seriously?" She let out a laugh.

"Nothing's funny."

"It's hilarious. What kind of question is that?"

"Skye, stop joking around and answer me."

"Yes, Desmond, I loved you. I still love you. I'll always love you, and that's the truth."

"Then why?" I push my plate away and lean back. "What was it about him that made you say fuck what we were building?"

I wasn't afraid to show her I'd been hurting. Her choosing to start over with another man made me question whether I was meant for her. I'd never been jealous or insecure, but when it came to Skye, I was all that shit. I had to be her everything; I wanted to be all she needed. The fact that another man so easily caught her attention fucked with me because what I felt for her was instant, and knowing she experienced that instant connection with another man fucked with me.

"Are we doing this?" She asks, rubbing her head.

"Yes, put it out there. Tell your truth, Ayla."

"Oh, you're using middle names…we're doing this," she says, taking a deep breath. "You might want to grab a drink."

"Nah, I'm good. I want to be sober for this. If you need a drink to acknowledge that you left me for another nigga go for it."

Skye is taking her sweet time answering the question, but I wait patiently, prepared to have my ego crushed.

"He was supposed to be a one-night-stand, okay?" She screams. "I was supposed to use him to get over you for the night, but I went back for more."

My chest feels like it's caving in as she speaks. I'm sick. The thought of another man fucking away her feelings for me is the closest one can get to death.

"He was giving me everything I needed you to give me. Sex, a shoulder to cry on, a listening ear. He opened up to me and communicated with me. He got me out of the cave I had crawled into, and the only way I could stay out of the darkness was to leave you." She exhales and lays her head down on the table.

"Skye," I say, getting up from the table because I officially have to drink something, "you could have talked to me."

"Desmond, are you being for real?" She stands from the table and follows behind me. "You were doing everything *but* speaking to me. You became cold and distant."

"I was grieving," I blurt out, then sip the beer I just opened. "Want one?" I ask her.

"You weren't the only one," she responds, taking the beer, "I was grieving too, and even though I was wrong, I thought you were cheating. It made it easier for me to pull away."

"Cheating isn't even in my vocabulary. You should have known that. You are my person. I had plans for us, for our family. I was excited to become a father. To raise a mix of the best parts of us. I was committed to you and no one else. I'm still committed to you despite everything that's happened." I walk toward the balcony, taking Skye by the hand and dragging her behind me. "I'm sorry I ran away every chance I got instead of being present. It was fucked up, and you didn't deserve it, so I understand why it was easy to fall into another man, but I'd be lying if I said I wasn't pissed off." I say, sitting on the swinging chair.

"You're not wrong. My heart would have broken had you moved on without me." Skye looks directly into my eyes.

"Moving on from you is impossible." I place my hand under her chin. "You're the only one for me. I should have fought harder for us, and I should have run after you that day."

"I should have never walked away." Skye takes hold of my face, tears forming in her eyes. "I've regretted it every day, but you told me not to come back."

"I never wanted you to leave in the first place. I was hurt. Those words meant nothing. I always want you to come back to me. You're my world, Skye. I love you and only you." I wrap my arms around her and pull her close, my eyes lowering to her lips.

"I love you too, Desmond, but I have a question." She stares up, and I can see the reluctance on her face.

"What is it?"

"Would you still want me back if I had decided to have his baby?"

"Baby… no baby…you're mine, and anyone you love, I love. I would have happily played stepdaddy," I place my hand on her chin and lift her head, "but I'd rather you go half on a baby with me and only me."

"Would you be fine with waiting?"

"I'll wait as long as I need to," I reply. "Can I kiss you now?"

"I thought you'd never ask," she says, wrapping her arms around my neck. Our lips collide, and we melt into one another.

<u>32</u>

Why Not

Friday, February 25, 2011

Skye

"So, did you two…you know?" Emily leans in close.

"No, I don't know."

She eases closer to me from across the table and whispers, "Fuck."

"You couldn't wait to ask me that question, could you?" I push her back and giggle. "Just nosy as hell."

"I'm a very patient person. I'm still waiting for an answer." In anticipation, Emily stares at me and taps her fingers on the dining table. "But I *cannot* wait any longer."

"Does it matter if we did or didn't?"

"Skye," Emily shrieks louder than intended.

Throwing my head back in a fit of laughter, I finally answer her question. "If you must know," I pause, "we did…*not*."

"Why in the hell not?" Emily bangs her hand on the table. "And if you didn't let him fuck you into oblivion, why the hell are you so damn happy? I only look like that when I've been—"

Emily stops mid-sentence to see if her remaining customers are in earshot, "—dicked down in a hundred different ways," she whispers as if she hadn't just blurted out the **F** word a minute prior.

Throwing my head back, I laugh.

"The thought of that beautiful man eating me out with his grill in, letting my juices moisturize his beard, and then having my back blown out crossed my mind numerous times, but we agreed to wait."

"Bitch," she yells, and the two women finishing up their shrimp and grits giggle. "I'm sorry, ladies." She blushes in embarrassment. "Seriously, what are you waiting on? You've got the guy you truly want, and you're *waiting*. I would have jumped Jordan's bones when his lips touched mine."

"I'm not sure I'm ready to be intimate just yet. I've touched myself. Shit, I did it as he watched, and you know what he did after I told him I wanted him?"

"You did what?" Emily smacks my hand. "Why didn't you tell me?"

"I was so fucking mortified. I put myself out there, and he denied me."

"But did he? Knowing Des, he had a reason for turning you away. So what was it?"

Rolling my eyes, I take a deep breath. "I hate that you know me so well, but he said if he crossed that line with me, I wouldn't be able to get rid of him, and we needed to hash some of our issues out."

"Alright, and you guys have officially done that. So what's the holdup? You weren't afraid to play in that little kitty in front of him with yo nasty ass." Emily giggles.

"Fuck you," I say with a smirk. "The thought of letting another man between my legs is scary. What if it's different?"

"Girl, the man lived between those legs for years. How different can it be?"

"I cannot take you." I fling my hands in the air. "Different as in our sexual chemistry might be off. It has been over a year since our last time together."

"And for that year, that man has been celibate. I'm sure he is ready to release all that sexual tension on you *and* in you." Emily makes a pumping gesture with her hands. "You on birth control?"

"Definitely on birth control, and you a damn lie." I lean forward, staring Emily down.

When they told me the man hadn't cheated on me, I accepted it, but I don't know if I believe his dick hasn't taken a swim in at least one other woman.

"Please believe it. Jordan tried to get him out there multiple times, and all he wanted to do was stay in the house, crying about how he lost you. It was getting pretty damn pitiful if you ask me, but Desmond loves *you*. We know it, and so does everyone else. You're his ending and his beginning. That man would get down on one knee and marry you within the same hour if it were up to him."

"You think so?"

"I know so," Emily says as she kisses my hand. "Now, can we celebrate that I won't have to chop my tits off? Isn't that why you came to see me?"

"Those lovely tits of yours," I say, leaning over to squeeze them.

While I was away having the worst and best time of my life, Emily found out the lump she felt in her breast was merely a cyst. Since the cyst wasn't causing her pain and appeared to be going away on its own, the doctor advised against a procedure. Emily needs to keep checking for any changes, but she seems in the clear when it comes to cancer.

"Not in front of the customers, Skye," she squeals.

"Those girls walked out of here somewhere between you bringing up my little kitty and you fucking the air." I mimic her gestures, causing her to burst into laughter.

"If that's the case, squeeze them again and feel around for any lumps while at it."

"You don't have to ask me twice," I say, returning my hands to her breast. "By the way, when do you plan on having this extravagant wedding of yours? I've heard nothing about it since the Christmas Eve party."

"I don't."

"What do you mean you don't? You've been dreaming of this for as long as I've known you. You have an entire vision board dedicated to your wedding day."

Removing my hand from her breast, Emily stands up and goes to the back toward her office. She returns with a bottle of champagne and her phone.

"I have something else to tell you." She sits beside me.

"See, now you're scaring me. Do I need to give Jordan a piece of my mind? Better yet, my fist?" I say, balling up my fingers.

"If you don't sit your little ass down. Jordan and I are doing better than ever," Emily says as she pops the bottle and begins to pour our drinks.

"Then what, Em? Stop making me wait."

"Who's the impatient one now," she says, handing me a glass.

"Oh, shut up and spill the tea."

"Better yet, let me show you."

Handing me her phone, I have to take a triple take. Emily and Jordan are standing at a rose-covered altar. She's wearing a red off-the-shoulder wedding dress with a 3D rose design and a long train. Her veil is black, far from what I visualized her wearing. Jordan is wearing a black and red 3-piece suit, and his hair—he cut his fucking hair. I was getting used to that silky ass hair he constantly had up in a bun.

"Bitch," I pause, "you got married without me, *and* you didn't wear a bright white princess dress...a-an and Jordan's hair... you got him to cut his fucking hair?"

"He looks good as fuck, right?" she says, smiling from ear to ear.

"You're a wife?" I shake my head and blink my eyes repeatedly.

"I'm a wife," she says, lifting her hand to show off her new vintage wedding ring.

"I'm so fucking happy for you," I say, almost dragging her across the table to hug her. "I should beat your ass for doing this without me."

"I know. I'm sorry. It was a spare-of-the-moment idea. I was over waiting, and I didn't need to have some big audience there to prove how much Jordan loves me. What we have is so special, and I wanted to keep that moment between us, and you know his ass wasn't going to object."

"I love you," I say, pulling Emily back for a hug.

"Bitch, are you crying?" Emily pulls away from me.

"Shut up and let me have this moment."

33

Date Night

Friday, May 27, 2011

Skye

Desmond finally cashed in on that rain check. It's five months late, but at least it's finally happening again.

We didn't want to start our new relationship where we left off—in each other's space, not speaking to one another, remaining comfortable, and not taking the time to communicate our wants and needs. I needed him to see me this time, even when I did my best to hide from him. I needed him to open up the parts of him he hid away because they made him seem weak. Our shit wouldn't always be tight, but if we were going to come together as one, I needed us to start right and continue until the end of time.

When he told me he wanted to take me out, I was nervous…excited but nervous. The last actual date we had happened a month before our tragedy. He took me to a cooking class, saying I needed to learn to whip up something more than noodles for his baby—*such a jerk. I can cook.*

Desmond didn't tell me where we were going, but I'm guessing it'll be fancy since he wants me to wear a sexy little black dress and red bottom heels. I hope he knows he'll be carrying me by the end of the night.

Desmond: *Be there in 30 minutes. I can't wait to be in the presence of an Angel.*

Skye: *Have you always been this sweet?*

Desmond: *Probably not lol.*

Skye: *Remind me why I like you again.*

Desmond: *Because I'm sexy as hell, make you laugh, and got good dick, but I'll remind you of that when the time is right.*

Skye: *You're right about one thing. You sure can make a woman laugh. See you in a little.*

Setting aside my phone, I concentrate on applying the final touches to my makeup— just a hint of blush and highlighter. I don't want to go overboard. With spring heading into summer, the temperature is rising, and I don't want my makeup to melt off my face.

Once I'm done, I stand in the mirror, taking one final look at myself. My hair is styled with precision, each strand falling perfectly into place—my dress clings to my small frame, accentuating my curves in all the right places. Confident in my appearance, I grab my phone and snap photos before Desmond texts me to come outside.

Damn, I look good. If he doesn't want to fuck me, I'll get the job done myself.

Desmond and I have yet to cross the point of no return. I've been taking things slow. I want to get back to my usual self without complicating an already complicated situation. We've come close but always hesitate, worried the other will pull away.

The doorbell rings, and suddenly, I feel nervous.

"Why am I nervous? I dated the man for four years," I say to myself in the mirror before grabbing my clutch.

I think about bringing a jacket, but it'll ruin my outfit. The drinks should keep me warm.

As I approach the front door, my nerves settle. Turning the knob and opening it, my heart skips a beat. There he is, standing handsome, with a warm smile. He's wearing a black tuxedo similar to the one he wore at the Christmas Eve party, and his black hair is neatly curled on the top of his head, the sides and back shaved low. This man is starting to change his hair more than me. I was getting used to the braids.

"You cut your hair?"

"Do you like it?" He asks.

"Did you and Jordan have some sort of pact?" I giggle.

"Woman," he attempts to hold in the smile forming on his face, "tell me you like it."

"I want to run my fingers through it," I say, feeling my cheeks redden.

"Save that for later. I spent hours perfecting these curls." He smirks. "Are you ready to ditch this place?"

"More than ready."

I lock the door, and Desmond gently takes me by the hand and leads me toward his car. Opening the door, he waits for me to take my seat and then puts on my seatbelt.

"I'm not a baby." I giggle.

"But *you* are…my baby." He winks before walking to the driver's side. Getting in the car, he hands me a silk eye cover and says, "Put this on."

"Desmond, do you know how long it took me to perfect this eyeliner?"

"I'm sure it'll be fine," he says, handing it to me. "Please wear it just this one time."

Snatching the eye cover from his hands, I gently place it over my eyes and relax into the seat.

"Any request?" Desmond asks.

"Hmm, put on something smooth, something sexy."

The soothing melodies of Usher fill the car, calming my mind and body. With each note, I sink into relaxation. Gently gliding his fingers up and down my thigh, Desmond says, "Don't be falling asleep over there."

"I'm just enjoying the ride."

About thirty minutes later, Desmond is escorting me out of the car and to our destination. Stopping, he carefully removes the cover from my eyes and places it in his pocket. We're standing in front of **The Vine**, this quaint Italian restaurant just outside town. It's where Desmond took me for our first official date—where he asked me to be his girlfriend—where we were supposed to be having that conversation about what happened between us.

On our first date here, I wore a black Forever 21 dress with a slight rip at the bottom. Emily did her best to fix it that night. I also wore cheap heels that were difficult to walk in, but Desmond pretended not to notice my struggle. I remember the slight smile on his face as I almost busted mine open in this exact spot.

"You didn't!" I beam and wrap my arms around his midsection, lifting my head, pushing out my lips, hoping he meets me with his—he does, and I latch on for as long as I can.

The atmosphere is cozy and romantic, with dim lighting and soft music playing in the background, just like I remember.

There was no way he was looking for closure when he planned on coming here some months ago.

As the hostess escorted us to our table, I realized Desmond must have requested the table from our first date—toward the back of the restaurant near the window. It's more intimate and away from the crowd. *He wants my undivided attention tonight.* Our first date set the tone for our relationship, full of warmth, laughter, and good food. I hope tonight is the start of something that'll last forever.

Pulling out my chair, Desmond ensures I am sitting comfortably before moving to his seat.

"I can't believe you were able to get the same table." I smile at him warmly, reaching my hands across to touch his. "How long have you been planning this?"

"That's my little secret." Desmond winks and interlocks his fingers in mine.

"Whatever, I already know what I want to order," I say as I see the waiter approaching.

Slipping from my grip, Desmond picks up the menu. "You sure you don't want to take a moment to look at all the options in front of you?"

"Nope!" I snatch the menu from his hand and give it to the waiter. "We'll have the spaghetti carbonara and your best red wine bottle. Thank you!"

"I can't believe my eyes." Desmond pauses in disbelief. "That's supposed to be my job. Are you paying too?" He smirks.

"Ha, definitely won't be digging in my wallet for this one." I laugh. "But it seems like we're reliving our first date, and if that's the case, I can clearly remember you drooling over the items on the menu for a good twenty minutes, and I had to end up ordering for the both of us."

"Hey, they have a lot of options. I still want to try that Chicken Parmesan over the creamed lemon ravioli." He licks his lips, making my pussy tingle, causing me to clench my legs together.

I should have worn panties.

"Next time," I promise him.

"So, does that mean I'll get a second date?"

"And a third if you play your cards right." I slip off my heel and glide my foot across his center. I watch him flinch in his chair, causing me to laugh.

"Naughty girl," he says, licking his bottom lip.

As the night went on, we laughed and talked for hours. Our food was delicious—creamy, savory, and perfectly cooked. We ordered a second bottle of red wine, primarily for me, and toasted to our re-found connection. We finished our meal with a decadent tiramisu and walked out onto the bustling streets.

~

Desmond

As the valet service retrieves my car, I feel Skye's delicate fingers moving through my hair as she rests on my back. Her touch is gentle, but I can tell she's had too much to drink when she tightens her grip on my curls.

"Save that aggression for the bedroom," I say, rubbing her leg.

"Who said you're even going to make it there?" She yanks my hair.

"Damn it, woman," I say, trying to unravel her fingers, "that hurt."

I hear her laugh as she caresses my head. "I'm sorry, you big baby. Let me make it better."

Though I love her playfulness, I'm praying she sobers up quickly. I don't want her to miss out on what I've planned. I have one more surprise in store for her.

"Time to get down." I attempt to get Skye off my back.

"No, I like it up here."

"I can tell. That little kitty is heating up back there." I chuckle.

"Oh shut up," she says, hitting me upside the head. "Put me down…*carefully,*" she warns.

The valet pulls up right as I put her down. Opening her door, she gets in the car, and I tip the valet before getting in.

"Where to next?" Skye leans over and whispers in my ear before licking my lobe. The feel of her wet tongue pressed against my earlobe has my dick on an escape mission.

"Simmer down, little lady. You'll see when we get there." I turn to kiss her and then focus back on the road.

"Pull over," she says, moving her hand to my zipper. "I know you want to be inside me."

"More than ever, but we're on a schedule," I say, placing my free hand on top of hers. *That wine got her feeling good.*

"It'll be quick," she moans into my ear.

"Ain't nothing going to be quick about what I'm going to do to you. I promise it'll be worth the wait."

"At least let me taste you."

I want to tell her, no, but I remain silent. I can see the look in Skye's eyes when I glance over at her. They're hungry, and she's waiting for me to feed her. Resting on her knees in the passenger seat, she undoes my pants, pulling out my dick.

"That shit is so damn beautiful and solid as a rock," she says, caressing me, causing an unexpected moan to fall from my lips. "You sure you don't want to pull over?"

Her hand is smooth to the touch. Softer than the last time she had them roaming my sensitive skin. She hasn't even placed her lips around the tip, and I'm ready to explode.

Don't embarrass yourself like that man.

"I can't," I respond, trying to remain relaxed.

"I know he misses me," she says, licking the precum flowing from the tip, swirling her tongue in circles before swallowing me whole. The sensation surprises me, and I slightly swerve into another lane.

Focus.

My seed shoots into the back of her throat just as I park the car. We had a slightly long drive to our second destination, and I had to think of everything possible in order not to explode before I stopped the car. That deep throat, tongue combo she was putting on me was going to be the death of us if I had to wait a second longer. Resting my head back, I jerk in my seat as Skye makes sure she's emptied me.

"You good?" she sits up, pulling down the passenger side mirror to make sure there's no evidence of me lingering on her lips.

"Better than ever," I say, adjusting myself into my pants. "Now, take this mint and kiss me. Don't want your breath smelling like my dick while you're talking to these people in there." I smirk.

"Shut up and hand me three of those," she says, putting her hand out.

I pull out my phone and send a quick text.

Desmond: *Yo, we're outside.*

Jordan: *Nigga, I said text me when you're leaving the restaurant.*

Desmond: *My bad, I got tied up.*

Jordan: *You a nasty ass nigga*

Desmond*: Man, shut up. If I'm not inside in 5 minutes... abort mission.*

~

Skye

I don't realize we're in front of the frat house across from the college campus because I'm too busy wondering who Desmond's texting. I just gave him the best head I've ever given while in a moving car, and all he does is hand me a breath mint.

We agreed on no phones for the night, and now I'm watching him text back-to-back with someone with an anxious look on his face.

Is some bitch trying to snatch him up?

We haven't exactly announced to anyone that we've been back together officially for some months now. On top of that, we still haven't had sex. He might be tired of waiting. I want to say something, but the night has been going well, and I refuse to ruin it with jealousy. If Desmond truly wanted to be with another woman, he would be. He could snap his fingers, and a flock would appear.

Snap out of it, Skye.

"I know we're reliving our first official date night…"

"You didn't suck the soul out of me with that pretty mouth on our first official date," Desmond states, putting his phone in his pocket.

"Too much?"

"Not enough," he admits, gliding his thumb across my bottom lip. "I can't wait to get you home."

"We can go now."

"Patience, my love. Don't you want to have some fun?" He questions.

"I know this is where we first met, but how much fun can we have partying with a bunch of kids? In these damn torturous heels at that," I respond, slipping my heels back on.

"Don't be boring. Plus, I have a solution for that." Desmond pops his trunk and gets out of the car. Walking around to my door, he opens it and brandishes my favorite pair of black walking shoes.

"Hey, I thought someone stole those," I yell excitedly, trying to snatch them from his hand.

"More like you left them in my car before you left me for that nigga."

"Really? I thought we hashed that out."

"We did." He laughs and kneels, placing my feet on his knee. Slipping off my shoes, he rubs my toes before putting my walking shoes on.

"Such a gentleman," I say, gently rubbing his face.

"I'm trying to be much more than that," he says, taking my hand to escort me out of the car. As we begin tracking toward the door, he stops. "One second, I forgot something."

I walk toward the door but stop because I'd rather head to his place.

"We can just—"

The words don't escape my lips because when I turn to face Desmond, he is on one knee, holding out an oval-cut diamond ring.

"Skye," he says, taking my hand once I walk closer to him. "You are more than just my girlfriend. You are the very essence of my being. Every moment spent with you is a treasure that I hold dear in my heart, and having to go all those days, weeks, and months without you almost caused me to end my life…"

Is this happening? Is he asking me to be his? To carry his last name and be his for a lifetime?

I dreamed of this moment the day I walked into this very house and locked eyes with him. I knew he was the one I wanted to spend the rest of my life with.

"…I cannot imagine a future without you in it, and it is my greatest hope that we can continue to grow old together, hand in hand, creating a life full of love and laughter. I understand that the idea of marriage is overwhelming," he pauses, gazing up at me with love in his eyes. I can't stop the tears from falling from mine, "but I want you to know that my love for you is not conditional on marriage. Whatever your decision, I will always be here for you as your man and friend. I want us to continue to grow and build a life together at a comfortable pace for both of us..."

"Shut up," I yell, pulling him off the ground. "I will be your wife...today, tomorrow, this year, and the next. Just put the ring on my finger already," I say, hugging him and dousing his face with kisses.

"You're going to have to back up off me first." We both laugh as I back up to let him up for air.

"Skye Ayla Rose..."

"Desmond Alexander Walker," I respond.

"Will you do me the honor of becoming my wife?"

"I said yes already," I say, putting out my hand, but he smacks it away. "I, Skye Ayla Rose, would love to become Mrs. Skye Walker."

"That's more like it," he says, kissing my hand before placing the ring on my finger.

I can't stop staring at my hand. The diamond on my engagement ring sparkles even at night. It's everything I ever wanted in a ring and more. As I turn my hand this way and that, I can see the excitement written on Desmond's face. This ring is the beginning of our never-ending journey in this unpredictable world.

"Oh, hush." I kiss him. "Let's go inside. I know it's another surprise in there for me."

Stepping through the door, I'm met with a burst of excitement from familiar faces, including my mom and dad.

Was this his intention all along? Was Desmond already planning to propose before we split?

A chorus of cheers and enthusiastic exclamations of "Congrats!" fills the air, and my heart leaps joyfully.

I gaze around the room, taking in the sight of all the beaming faces before me. I feel gratitude wash over me, knowing that these wonderful people gathered together to celebrate our love. I draw deep breaths and walk further into the room, basking in the warmth and affection radiating from every corner. This moment will forever be etched in my memory.

"When this night is over, I'm going to fuck you like it's my last day on Earth," I whisper to Desmond.

<u>34</u>

The Hangover

Saturday, May 28, 2011

Desmond

So much for getting fucked.

It sounded nice, but I knew that wasn't about to happen. Skye did the complete opposite of sobering up—she drank like we were college students with no care in the world. Throwing back drink after drink knowing she's a lightweight.

The second she jumped on the table and declared to the room she was related to Beyoncé, it was time to go home. By then, her parents had already left for their hotel room. Thank goodness. Lina would have had a field day had she witnessed her daughter's wild and drunken side.

Jordan and Emily got a kick out of watching me struggle to get Skye to the car. If there were a bucket of popcorn around, they would have been eating it with a sparkle in their eyes. Every time I got close to getting her out the door, a new song came on, another drink was in her hand, and she was chanting, "Bitch I'm a wife." I needed to get her home before it got worse.

"You sure that's the woman you want to marry," Emily joked as Skye clung to the doorframe with a death grip.

I forgot how strong that little ass woman is.

"Absolutely," I informed her.

There has never been any doubt regarding how I feel about Skye—my beginning and ending—the only person I want to do life with.

After everything she's been dealing with—the miscarriage, our breakup, another breakup, and the end of another pregnancy, it brought me joy to experience her more carefree side—to see her let go of the pain she's been trying to hide.

Seeing her drunk, not giving a care in the world, brought back memories of me having to throw her tiny frame over my shoulder every time she wanted to stay at a house party past party hours. She took advantage of her last two years of college. Making sure she attended as many functions as she could because she refused to before meeting me. Then there were the nights she spent hours singing karaoke until she finally passed out on the floor.

Once Skye was in her zone, nothing could stop her, but that's what I always loved most about her. She was dedicated to everything she did, including proving she could hang with the big dogs all night, knowing she couldn't.

"God, it feels like someone knocked me in the head with a bat. I'm pretty sure the room is spinning," Skye says, walking into the kitchen, holding one hand to her head, and rubbing her lower back. "Did we get into a fight or something?" She stretches.

"The only person you got in a fight with is the liquor, and I think you know who won."

"Oh my god, why didn't you stop me?" She staggers into the living room and drops

on the enormous bean bag in the corner. "I
feel like I'm dying."

"Baby, you look like it." I laugh. "I have
just the cure. That's if you have the energy
to get up."

"Can't we just stay in bed and watch
movies all day in the dark?" She lifts her
head from the floor, "Please. My world is
spinning."

"And miss out on lunch with your
parents?"

This morning, Skye's mother sent me a
message asking if we could meet before
they headed home. I knew Skye wouldn't be
comfortable spending the day pretending to
get along with her, but I didn't say no.
Instead, I promised to try to see if she'd be
feeling up to it without making any
concrete plans. That was until her dad
called my phone and scared the hell out of
me.

Last night, she and Lina had little
interaction, so I don't even want to imagine
them sitting down for a serious
conversation today. I was hesitant about

inviting her to the surprise engagement party, but I didn't want Skye to have any regrets when she thought back to the night I proposed. She might not admit it, but I saw that sparkle in her eyes when they landed on her parents.

I'm hoping Skye can work through her issues with her mother—I don't want to push her too hard, but when you don't have living parents, you tend to look at situations like these differently. I'd hate for us to get to our wedding day, and they're still in a place where they want to rip out each other's throats over the slightest thing.

"Absolutely not. Please tell me you didn't agree to it." She yawns.

"I figured that would be your response…but you need to be the one to call and tell her we can't make it," I say, walking in her direction with a cup of coffee. "You two will have to sort out your issues eventually."

Lifting, Skye crosses her legs and takes the coffee from my hand. "Today isn't going to be that day. I have a massive headache, and I don't even want to think about how she's going to make it worse." Skye sips her coffee. "I can see her now, pretending to be so happy, acting as if she's proud of me when she told me I had no goals just a few months ago."

"Your parents, your decision, but think about it."

"No need. I'll call my dad and tell him we won't be able to make it."

"And while you do that, I'm going to run to the store and grab some groceries." I lean down to kiss her.

What I'm really about to do is grab her some food for that dreaded hangover she has, then meet up with her dad. Once Skye calls him, I'll give her mom the go-ahead. She's hanging close by. I pray to God and all the heavens that Skye doesn't call off the engagement once all of this is over, but I knew if I gave her a heads up, she'd be out of there at the speed of light, and her dad would have my head on a stake because of it.

~

Skye

Building up the courage *and* energy to call my dad isn't an easy task. The call should be quick, but I don't want to make it. They came all this way to celebrate my engagement, and I'm blowing him off because I can't stand to be around my mom.

I can hear the sweetness in my dad's voice singing my mother's praises through the phone. Telling me how much she's been looking forward to spending time with me and congratulating me again on my engagement without a crowd of people being around.

It'll be hard to resist.

All I want to do is lay under my fiancé for the rest of the day while he does all he can to cure this dreadful hangover of mine. I don't think coffee, food, or medication will fix this.

I make another cup of coffee anyway and grab a bagel from the top of the fridge. The point of him leaving was so he could come back to cook, but I'm starving. If I don't put something in my stomach now, he's going to come home to a dead woman, and there goes becoming Mrs. Skye Walker.

The jokes that will come with my newfound name will be ridiculous. *In all* the years of dating Desmond, I never thought about what it would be like for our names to be combined until Emily and Jordan started making Star Wars references last night. Speaking of last night, I promised Desmond the ride of his life, and I couldn't even do that. I'm not sure what made me think I could party as hard as I did last night, but I don't have it in me. I never really did.

Once I stuff my face with a bagel covered in jam and cream cheese and chug my coffee, I pick up my phone to call my dad.

"Dad," I say into the phone sweetly.

"I was wondering when you'd call."

"I won't be able to make it to lunch with you and mom. I have the absolute worst hangover."

"I'm sure you do, sweetheart, but it's too late."

"What do you mean it's too late?"

"She should be knocking on the door right about…now."

On cue, I hear a knock at Desmond's door, and my heart drops. What is he? A lawyer and a got damn magician?

"Dad…"

"Sorry, sweetheart, but I'm tired of you and your mom's shit. I knew you would try to talk your way out of this one, but I've dealt with you and your mom's bullshit long enough. I know she's tough on you. She's always been a feisty one and one to go against everything your grandmother wanted for her. She didn't want you to do the same, and she went about it in the wrong way. I'm sorry I always minded my business when it came to how she treated you, but It's time you two start new, and while you do that, I'll be holding your little fiancé hostage."

"But dad…"

My mom knocks at the door again.

"Answer the damn door, girl. I promise she won't take long to say what she needs to. Whether you choose to forgive her is all up to you, but baby girl, something's gotta give."

"Fine. For you," I huff.

"Love you, baby girl.

"Love you too, Dad."

Desmond: *Sorry...your dad's one scary man.*

I don't bother texting Desmond back. I know how terrifying my father can be when he's sick and tired, and it's clear he's tired. If he weren't, my mother wouldn't be at Desmond's door trying to work our relationship out. I put my hand on the doorknob. Hesitant to turn it. She bangs again—more demanding this time.

"Skye Ayla Rose."

I open the door. "Come on in."

"Does Desmond have some bowls and silverware?" She asks, walking through the door without so much as a hi. "I brought you something for that hangover. Foe."

"Pho," I correct her.

"Whatever it's called, I got it. Point me to the goods, and you sit your pretty self down."

"I'm sure the last thing I look is pretty," I respond, guiding her with my pointer finger to where the glass bowls and silverware are.

I can smell the spices and beef broth as she pulls the pho out of the bag. Desmond probably placed the order for her and handed it to her himself. She wouldn't dare be caught buying noodle soup in public.

"You're always pretty. You are my daughter," she says, walking to the dining table. "Ya look just like me."

Maybe that's why you're such a bitch to me.

I'm happy to see the pho is still piping hot. This will cure my hangover and get me through this conversation, which might not be so bad.

"That's nice of you to say, but you can be honest."

"Skye," she sits across from me, "I know you think I'm here to scold or throw petty remarks at you, but I promise you I'm only here to make things right between us. I know I've been a terrible mother."

"I couldn't agree more," I say, sipping the broth. It tastes so good going down.

"I'll take that. My way of showing you how much I care hasn't been the most conventional."

"Oh, ya say." I slurp a noodle into my mouth.

"So, this is how this conversation is going to go?" She stands. "You're going to give me sarcastic responses every time I say something?"

She thought she could walk in here with my favorite hangover food, tell me how pretty I am, and then expect everything to return to how it was before I became a teenager. Those were supposed to be the years we became the closest, but we just seemed to drift further and further from each other the older I got.

I saw it in her eyes the moment I opened the door. I know she's wondering why I smell like the night before and have my hair tossed in an atrocious bun—there are probably still traces of mascara and eyeliner smudged across my eyes. She's probably wondering why Desmond would want to marry a woman who can't even look *presentable*.

She stares at me with her hands on her hips, waiting for me to say something. Something like I know you love me, and I forgive you, but I don't forgive her—not yet.

We have issues.

I'm not entirely sure what those issues are, but they won't be fixed today. It will take a lot of apologizing and possibly a therapist to get us back on track. That's not something I'm sure she'll agree to.

I let her stand there in silence as I finish the rest of my pho—not speaking until every last drop is gone.

"Skye," she yells once I put the bowl down. "I'm trying to fix things."

"No, you're just trying to appease Dad. It took him being fed up watching the two women he loves more than anything going at it." I stand up and walk the bowl over to the sink. I continue to talk as I rinse it out. "Would you have even come here today if he and Desmond didn't set this up?"

"Uh," she hesitates, "of course."

"You're lying, Mom." I walk over and grab her hand, leading her to the couch. "And that's okay. I'm not ready to lay all our problems out on the table, and I'm damn sure not ready to sweep them under the rug."

"But—"

I interrupt her before she can finish speaking because I don't know when I'll have another opportunity to speak my mind like this.

"You hurt me. You've been hurting me for almost half of my life, and do you know, out of those ten years, you've probably only apologized to me twice? Twice for the millions of times you've belittled me, disrespected me, and made me feel like I'm unworthy of *everything*."

I gaze at her to see if she feels any remorse for the way she's treated her one and only child, but she looks empty inside. For a woman who seems to have it all—her eyes tell a different story.

She takes my hands in hers. "And I'm so sorry for that, but this is the only way I know how to be. It doesn't mean I don't love you. You are literally a miracle, and I know I should have treated you as such, but I've always been scared I'd lose you."

"So you push me away instead?"

"No, I forced you to be strong, resourceful, and determined." she balls my hand into hers. "I made you into the wonderful woman you are today."

"Is that what you think you've been doing?" I remove my hands forcefully. "You practically broke me. I'm the woman I am today because I didn't want to turn into the one sitting in front of me. I would never treat my children the way you've treated me. Thank goodness you picked a standup guy like my dad, or I would have been completely fucked."

"Language," my mom responds. "I'm sorry you feel that way, but I would like to come to some kind of understanding."

"Mom, this isn't a business deal. I'm your daughter, and you need to work extremely hard to regain my trust. I love you, but I don't agree with how you treat me. If you want to go to some family counseling or start planning to spend genuine mother-daughter time with me, I'm open, but I need you to be open too, not because Dad told you to."

My mother says nothing—she leaps forward and locks me in her arms. She holds onto me tight. Longer than she ever has before. I let myself relax into her, appreciating a moment I may never get again.

"I promise I'll do better," she whispers. "You just wait and see."

And with those words, she kisses my cheek and exits.

Skye: *I'd kill you if I didn't love you so much. Get your scary ass back home lol.*

<u>35</u>

A New Beginning

Saturday, May 28, 2011
Skye

Desmond: *Seriously! You play too much.*

Skye: *That's what you get for not telling me my mom was waiting for me outside your place the whole time.*

The minute my mom left, I sent Desmond a text, hurried into a pair of his sweats, a hoodie, and my black sneakers, then walked the two blocks back to my place—using the extra set of keys he had sitting in the glass bowl on top of his minibar to lock up.

The food my mother brought gave me just the right amount of energy to make my way home without feeling like I was going to be sick. The fresh air was a bonus, filling me with the life that had drained from me the night before.

It had been a while since I'd walked through our beautiful neighborhood—taking in the smell of fresh maple and lavender drifting from the trees surrounding me. The mix of the two aromas calmed me, making me forget that only moments ago, I had been in an intense conversation with my mother—one of the reasons I left Desmond's. I wanted to avoid having to talk about it.

I know his intentions were pure. I know he wants what's best for me. I know he knows my heart and how much I'd regret not having my mom a part of my new life, but I need a moment to myself. To gather my thoughts. To decide if I truly want to take that step to mend my troubled relationship with her.

I'm sure he understands.

I should do this more often, I think, as I inch closer to home. I've always been so quick to rely on my car that I've forgotten how therapeutic a simple walk can be.

Desmond attempts to get me out of the comfort of my bed and out into the world, telling me I'm going to go blind and become paralyzed if I stay in one place—in the dark for too long. I even tried attending his fitness classes a few times since we've gotten back together but quickly figured out it isn't for me. I can barely make it through my hot yoga classes, so there is no way in hell I'll ever make it through a two-hour boot camp, which clearly isn't for beginners.

Looking at the houses I'm passing, I stop and think about where Desmond and I will live.

Has he been saving up money? Are we going to be stuck in an apartment forever? Or will I get to move into a home as beautiful as the one I'm staring at?

Despite getting back together and me saying yes to being his wife, we haven't discussed much about our living situation, and we haven't talked about bringing any babies into this world—at a point in time, it was all I could think about.

Now that I'm thinking about it, my mom is just *one* of the many obstacles to making our future together successful.

Desmond: Is that any way to treat your future husband? And tell me you've made it home.

On cue, Desmond texts me when I put my key into the door. The walk was faster than I remembered, or I was just too deep in my thoughts to realize how fast I'd been walking.

Skye: Serves you right lol. Thanks for the food, though, sweetcakes. I'm walking into my place now.

Once I text him back, I step into my apartment and lock the door behind me.

It feels good to be home.

I instantly get to lighting candles. I turn on the TV and switch to the music station—doing all I can to keep my mind steady—off anything heavy.

I can't wait to shower. Then I'm going to take a nice hot bath and lay in bed naked for the rest of the day. But first I need to clean my room.

Clothes are lying across the bed and floor. Despite being clean, I scoop them up and toss them in the laundry basket. I'm too lazy to think about folding and hanging them back up. I would have cleaned this mess before leaving the house if I knew I would be gone all night.

I toss my wash towels into the basket and grab a new one on my way into the bathroom. Of course, there's a ton of makeup that I didn't even use scattered all over the counter. I'm tempted to toss it in the trash, but I'll regret it later.

Forty minutes later, I'm lying across my bed, drifting off to sleep, but the sound of my doorbell quickly awakes me. *It must be Desmond here to make up for tricking me.* Rushing to the door, I swing it open, ready to jump into Desmond's arms.

It's about time I finally relieve some of this tension, and what's the best way of doing that than climbing on top of the man I'm going to spend the rest of my life with? I think he's waited long enough for this moment.

"I knew you couldn't stay away long."

As I'm about to drop my towel to bare all my glory to Desmond, hands quickly reach out and hold it in place.

"You don't want to do that."

The sound of Lance's voice startles me. I don't have to look up to know it's him. Shoving him back with one hand, I slam the door and rush to my room. *What is he doing here, of all places?* I haven't seen or spoken to him since he brought me home from the hospital—since we decided to go our separate ways.

Is it so hard to get a moment of peace? To spend a day celebrating my engagement with the one person I know was made for me. First, it was my mom, and now It's my ex. What the hell is going to happen next? I know it can't get any worse than this.

I take my time throwing on my lounging clothes, hoping Lance will just walk away, but then I hear a knock on the door. Whatever he has to say, he's willing to wait.

Today already isn't going my way, and I'd hate for Desmond to show up and see Lance standing at my door. I damn sure don't want him thinking I'm sneaking around on him. Grabbing my phone, I send Desmond a quick text before building the courage to walk back to the living room to face Lance.

Before exiting the room, my phone rings. "Do I need to come over there?" Desmond asks calmly. Calmer than I expected.

"No, I just wanted to tell you what's happening."

"Is he inside?"

"I haven't even opened the door back."

"What do you mean back?"

"Long story short. I heard the door, and I thought it was you. I opened it and almost dropped my tow—"

"Don't tell me you answered the door butt ass naked," Desmond cut me off.

"I said almost. He didn't see anything."

"You sure you don't need me to come over there? Make sure he doesn't try anything weird."

"Desmond."

"Yes."

"Do you trust me?"

"Of course I trust you. *Him*, I don't know."

"Well, trust me enough to see what this man wants before I send him on his way." The doorbell rings in the middle of my talking to Desmond, "It doesn't sound like he's going to walk away anytime soon."

"Alright," Desmond hesitates. "I love you."

"I love you more," I say before hanging up.

As I open the door, I see Lance walking away. I hesitate momentarily, wondering if I should call out his name. Then I realize there's nothing left to say. We decided to end things, and I thought we both found closure. There's no reason for him to speak to me again. There was no chance for us to rekindle what we had and no room for friendship. It's time for him to move on and let go of what once was.

I can't help but watch him walk away, knowing it's the last time I'll see him. But then, he stops and turns back towards me. His eyes speak volumes, regret etched in every line. I can tell he wants to say something that could change everything. But I can't let him. Life isn't a fairytale, at least not for Lance and me. Maybe he thought coming here would change things for us, but my life is heading in a new direction.

I lift my left hand, showing off the sparkling engagement ring on my finger. It symbolizes my love and commitment to the man I adore—I've loved since day one.

This is a new beginning for me, ending a chapter of my life that we can never undo.

<u>36</u>

What's Done is Done

Saturday, May 28, 2011
Lance

Last night, I was minding my business when Skye crossed my mind. I woke up and called my mom because no matter how upset she may have been with me, and yes, she was still upset about not becoming a grandmother, she always kept it real.

"Mom."

"Good morning, Son. What's got you ringing my line this early in the morning."

"Love," I admit.

"Oh, good. I thought you were calling about Skye," she says with relief.

"That's exactly who I'm calling about."

"So, I'm guessing you've heard the big news."

I have no clue what she's talking about, but I'm sure I'm about to find out. "I can't believe she's about to get married to that guy you were telling me about."

"She's what?" I roar through the phone.

"She got engaged last night," my mom informs me. "She was tagged in a ton of pictures on that Facebook last night. I thought you would have seen them by now."

Rushing into my room, I grab the laptop off my bed and log into Facebook. *Do I remember my password? I haven't been on there in ages. Everyone is so nosy, including my mom.* I don't even have to type in Skye's name because, as my mom said, there are pictures of her all over the home page, smiling and showing off her ring. *She's beautiful.*

"Son, you there? Are you okay?"

"Mom, I was calling because I wanted her back. I love her."

"I'm sorry, baby, but you're a day too late."

"But what if I'm not? What if she only said yes because I made her...you know...and then just disappeared."

"Do you love her the way your dad loved me?" She asks.

"I don't know. I might," I respond.

"If you don't, stay away from that girl. Let her be happy. You've already caused her enough pain." My mom pauses for a second before speaking again. "But if you do, you have to go after her, Son. Life is too short to wonder what could have been. If it doesn't work out, that's okay. At least you'll know you tried."

"I love you. Wish me luck."

"You're going to need more than that," she mumbles.

"What was that?"

"Love you too, Son."

~

Desmond

That's one sad-looking nigga, I think, as I approach Lance.

Skye said she didn't need me to come by but wasn't no telling what that nigga was up to. The last time they were in a room together, he was disrespectful as fuck. I should have whooped his rude ass. After getting off the phone with Skye, I thought about it. I just knew I couldn't allow him to pull that shit again, not with my woman.

From the look on his face, though, it didn't seem like she needed my help. Skye has always been able to handle herself. I can only imagine the words that came out of her mouth to make that man look like his whole world was ending.

Stopping in front of him, I ask, "What brings you here?"

"I was just in the neighborhood."

"Just in the neighborhood." I look around and nod my head. "And you just happened to end up at my woman's house?" I question. "You must have wanted something."

"Nothing important," he says, attempting to walk around me.

I step to the side, blocking his way. "It had to be kind of important for you to drive yo ass over here instead of making a phone call."

"Like I said," he sizes me up, "it wasn't nothing important...not anymore. What's done is done. Now, can you move the fuck up out of my way so I can go about my day? Or do we have a problem?"

I lift my hands and step back. *This nigga is mad as hell.* I would be, too, if I fumbled a woman as fine, driven, caring, and brilliant as mine.

"Desmond." I look past him and see Skye standing at the door. He turns around at the sound of her voice. "Is everything okay?"

"We're good," I say, placing my hand on Lance's shoulder. "Right?"

He pushes my arm away and says, "She's all yours."

"Long as you know. There's no get back when it comes to that one over there." I let my eyes shift to Skye. "So I hope you got every last word out that you needed to say because this will be the last time you get to pop up on my woman."

Lance takes one last look at Skye and then proceeds to walk away.

"I told you you didn't have to come over here," she says as I approach the door.

"And let that man think it's cool to pop up on you whenever he feels like it. I think the fuck not. You're mine," I say, picking her up and walking her inside. "We've got some movies to watch."

The End...is just the beginning.

Epilogue

Saturday, August 10, 2013

Skye

We're back in the place we decided we would start over again—leave all the hurt in the past and not forget what got us to where we are now—happily engaged...*still*—the Sea Ranch.

Yeah, I know, I should be married by now, but Desmond and I still had a shit load of luggage to unpack. Thanks to therapy, we've been able to do that. I could admit that I played a significant role in our demise. For so long, I put all the blame on him when I shouldn't have. Refused to speak up—be vulnerable.

Although therapy has allowed us to see our flaws and how we handle challenging and uncomfortable situations, we still have work to do. One thing we've prioritized is checking in with each other regularly, just as if we were running a business. I refuse to let misunderstandings and assumptions get in the way of our love. We both know from experience that it's easy to fall into the trap of silent suffering, so we are set on *never* letting that happen again.

Despite all the work we put into staying honest and committed to one another, it's been two years since Desmond got down on his knee and asked me to be Mrs. Walker. It's unbelievable how the time has just flown by—faster than I thought it would have. Everyone thought we'd run down the aisle to exchange "I do." We would have if Desmond could have had it his way, but I didn't want to rush. Rushing never got Desmond and me the outcome we truly wanted.

That doesn't mean I haven't let him tear my insides to shreds. It sounds painful, but it's the best sex we've ever had. Only God knows how I stayed off that ride for as long as I did. It took about four months for me to finally fuck him like it was our last day on earth. I don't know if it was the time we spent apart or the thought of another man doing to me what he hadn't for over a year, but Desmond put the dick on me so good I almost tatted his name more than once.

Emily was thrilled when I dragged her to the tattoo shop. I thought I could talk her into getting one with Jordan's name, but she refused to be stamped.

"The ring is enough," she told me, as I almost fainted at the sight of the tattoo gun. The sound hurt more than the actual tattoo.

Our double dates have been reinstated, which have momentarily satisfied Emily—trips to the islands, making an ass of ourselves on the basketball court trying to play two-on-two with our men, picnics in the park, and the occasional dinners I force her to come to at my parents' house. Even with all those distractions, it will not hold her off from planning my wedding.

I'm still not sure when we'll go down that aisle, but I assure you it will happen. I will kill Desmond before I let him get away. *Joking, but not.*

And yes, I've made it my duty to visit my parents as much as possible. The first time Emily and Jordan came to dinner with us was to see with her own two eyes the effort my mom has been putting in to be a better person. Emily had only ever witnessed the side of my mom that was highly critical and sometimes plain evil. She didn't believe me when I told her she had turned a new leaf.

Life is short, and it took talking to Desmond and my therapist to realize it. I'm truly blessed to have my mom and dad still. Some people wish they could get a redo to mend what was broken before they completely lost that chance. I still had one, and since my mom was trying desperately to show me that she wanted to be in my life the way I needed her to be, I figured it was time to stop fighting it.

She still gets on my nerves, but we aren't as bad as we once were. My dad has never been happier. He was convinced we would be the reason for his early departure. I didn't realize how much we both were stressing him out.

"Girl," Emily burst into the room. "What are you doing? Writing your damn life story? What's taking you so long?"

"Something like that," I respond, slamming my laptop shut.

"Well, that can wait for another time. I'm trying to enjoy my last bit of freedom before I pop this baby out." Emily rubs her stomach.

"You're lucky we even brought you here. This is supposed to be our secret spot. And didn't your doctor say you shouldn't be on your feet?" I get up and walk toward Emily.

"She said I shouldn't overexert myself, but I won't do that here. I just wanted one last double date with my friends. I'll sit back and let you all pamper me."

"Can't you just call it a weekend getaway? It's not a date."

"If I say it's a date, it's a date," Emily insists.

I kneel and start rubbing her stomach. I squeal when I feel a kick.

Emily smiles. "Yeah, I'm still not used to that," she says, placing her hand on top of mine and moving my hand down and to the left.

"We've got us a boxer in there," I smile.

"My daughter is not about to be in nobody's boxing ring. Get away from my stomach with that madness."

"God Mommy got you, baby. Gotta make sure you stay ready," I whisper into Emily's belly. "It's some weirdos in this world." She puts her hand on my head and pushes me away.

It took Emily a while to let me know she was pregnant. One day I showed up at her restaurant, and a tiny waist and a poking belly greeted me. I had to refrain from cussing her out in front of everybody. I couldn't believe she hadn't told me about her pregnancy. My slow ass should have known something was up. One day she stopped drinking cold turkey—something about her being on a diet, but her ass was eating everything in sight. The stomach came out of nowhere. A few weeks before, she was flat as a board. It's wild to me how a woman's body works.

We sat down, and she explained that she wasn't sure how to tell me about the good news without me feeling triggered. It was understandable. I had been through so much—a heartbreaking miscarriage and an abortion, that, at times, I regretted. I felt like a terrible person for going through with it, but by the time Emily had gotten pregnant, I was pretty much healed. I had my days, but life had been good.

I would have been ecstatic with the news if she'd told me sooner. She was finally getting everything she swore she would miss out on. I'm just happy she didn't hesitate to make me the godmother. I've gone to almost every appointment with her. The doctor was starting to think I was Jordan's second wife.

"Change into something comfortable. We're about to karaoke."

"Aren't you tired of doing that? You're not supposed to be dancing and jumping around," I respond.

"I am not you, Skye. The only person who puts on an entire concert is you, Miss

Beyoncé Jr. Now, hurry up," she says, turning around and returning down the steps.

I was not rushing downstairs, so I tucked my laptop away and showered. The guys can keep her busy while I get cleaned up. After putting on shorts, a tank, and a brown plaid button-up, I head downstairs.

Um, where is everyone?

I check the living room first, but it's empty, so I enter the entertainment room. That's empty as well.

"I do not feel like playing hide-n-seek with you grown-ass people. If Emily hurts herself because y'all want to be childish, I'm going to beat all of your asses."

I hear snickering as I get closer to the kitchen. No one's in there, so I walk toward the patio. Sliding the door open, I see a cake sitting on the table and balloons covering the ground. There's a pink banner that says, **Happy Birthday, Skye**.

"Happy birthday," Emily and Jordan yell.

"I bet you thought we forgot all about you," Emily says.

"Aww, thanks, guys. I kind of wish you did. I feel like I'm getting old."

As much as I enjoy celebrating holidays, my birthday is the one day I've never been fond of. I couldn't even tell you why. It's just one of those days that reminds me that life is constantly moving, whether I've accomplished everything I wanted to or not. Typically, I spend it alone, and those close to me know not to make a big deal.

I stop, look around, and notice Desmond isn't standing with them. "Where is my fiancé?"

"Can you still call him that after two years?" Emily questions, and Jordan lets out a roaring laugh. I cut my eyes at him, and he quiets immediately.

"Don't be mean to me on my birthday," I respond.

"You don't even like—"

I cut Jordan's statement short with one look, and Emily snickers.

"So, as I was saying, where is Desmond hiding?"

"You have to put this on first." Emily holds out a silk pink eye cover.

"Tell me you're joking," I say.

"My boy don't play when it comes to the blindfolds." Jordan laughs.

"You swear you're funny." I giggle.

"You're laughing, ain't you?"

"You make me laugh, babe," Emily says, kissing him on the cheek.

"Give me the damn thing," I snatch it from Emily's hand.

I think back to the day we had our first official date as a couple for the second time. That night was beautiful. Full of love and surprises. What could he be up to now? We're already engaged.

"Hurry up so I can find out what I got."

"So impatient." She shakes her pointer finger at me.

"Lead the way...and y'all bet not let me fall."

"You got it, princess," Jordan says.

Before I know it, I'm over his shoulder, and he's darting through the house.

"Wait for me," Emily yells.

"You bet not be running," I shout. "She bet not be running." I hit Jordan in the back and they both laugh.

We come to an abrupt stop, and I can feel the breeze hit me in the face.

"Man, if you don't put my woman down," Desmond says. He sounds like he is just a touch away.

"I was just trying to speed up the process," Jordan says, putting me down gently.

Desmond removes the cover from my eyes and wraps me in his arms. "Happy birthday, Wifey."

"Thank you, Hubby. What did you get me?"

"Straight to the point," he says, kissing me.

"Well, I know those things," I point to the eye cover, "always come with a surprise."

"You're right. Turn around."

I turn around to see a banner plastered across the front of the house. It says: **WELCOME HOME! I CAN'T WAIT TO MOVE.**

I turn back toward Desmond in disbelief. I just might faint. *How? We can't afford this place. We can't move here. It's too far away. I can't be far away from Emily and the baby.*

"Desmond Alexander Walker."

"I know, I know," he stops me, "we can't afford this place."

"So why did you—"

"I didn't." He hunches over, laughing, and I push him.

"Thank God. I was about to pass out. Why do y'all play so much." I hit him in the chest.

"Nah, but I did get you something." He pulls a black ring box from his pocket. "Open it."

Slowly opening the box, my heart beats with anticipation. *Did he upgrade my ring?*

I look up at Desmond, slightly confused. "A key?"

"Yes, baby, a key."

"To what," I ask, and Emily sighs loudly.

"Girl, are you slow?" She shouts, and Desmond laughs.

"It's a key to our new house in Maple, the one you can never stop looking at when we go for walks."

"But I thought someone bought it already," I respond in disbelief.

"Yeah, me, silly. I wanted to surprise you for your birthday."

As I gaze up at Desmond, my eyes fill with joy and gratitude. I leap into his arms, and he smiles before kissing me passionately. We embrace for what seems like an eternity. When I turn my head, Emily and Jordan are nowhere to be seen. I guess we were making out a little too long for them.

I'm overwhelmed with joy.

This key is not just any ordinary key. It symbolizes the start of a new chapter in our lives, new beginnings, and a future filled with hope and possibilities. We are on our way to building the life we dreamed of having since the beginning. With a ring and

a house, the only thing left is having a baby.
I can't wait.

"You want to make a baby," I say,
squeezing my legs tight around Desmond.

"You have to marry me first," he replies
with a wink.

"Okay," I agree.

Desmond yells towards the house,
"Emily!"

"Yes!" I see her standing at the door.

"She said yes," Desmond announces.

Before I could say anything, I heard
Emily's excited voice, "Grab the keys, get
the dress. We're having a wedding!"

My eyes widened in surprise. "Now?"

*A wedding! Right now? What if I had said
no?* These people are truly crazy, but I love
them. It's not like I have a reason to keep
pushing it off. I guess we're eloping.

"Yes, now!" Desmond and Emily say in
unison.

Best Birthday Ever!

The End…for real, this time

Thanks for reading!

Other Books by Sydney Reneé

<u>Related</u>
Our First Christmas: Skye and Desmond

<u>Women's Fiction</u>
Let's Be Friends
Let's Be Friends...Again
Let's Be Friends...Always

<u>Urban Fiction</u>
In Love with an Oakland Hot Boy
Emerald's Revenge: Sin in the City